Empty Houses

To order additional copies, please contact us.
BookSurge, LLC
www.booksurge.com
1-866-308-6235
orders@booksurge.com

Empty Houses
A Pastoral Approach to Congregational Closures

Michael K. Jones

2004

Empty Houses

Table of Contents

"All houses eventually become empty." Peter Berger, *Invitation to Sociology*

"The grass withers, the flower fades, but the word of our God will stand forever." Isaiah 40: 8*

*All scriptural quotations will be from the New Revised Standard Version.

To Trish - for all of the love, patience, and understanding to see me through this project.

Introduction

A couple of years ago I was asked to serve a congregation facing a difficult decision. They were preparing to decide whether or not they would remain open. It was a challenging time for both the parishioners and the wider denomination. The congregation was facing a number of challenges and realities that threatened its viability. These challenges ranged from financial pressures to declining attendance.

One afternoon, while serving this congregation, I found myself perusing the shelves of a local Christian bookstore. As I was reviewing the titles I quickly realized that there was a lot of material concerning church planting, growth and transition. There was little, however, about church closures. There were precious few resources that could help with the decision-making process and the conflicts these choices could generate. There was little that could help us minister to one another while people grieved the loss of their church home. It is a similar feeling to being unable to find a map before an important trip. We know where we may be going but we have little idea of how we're going to get there.

As a result of this fruitless search for resources a friend

suggested I write a book about what happened. As I considered the possibility I realized that the best option was the production of a resource that could help other congregations facing the possibility of closure. Albert Camus once began a book review with the words, "Today's writers talk about what happens to them."[1] Even though these words were penned over fifty years ago they still ring true today. "Empty Houses" is based on personal experience. It is also based on information found during the closure of the congregation I was serving at the time. "Empty Houses" is based on what happened during this process. It is also built on the hopes of what can happen in the lives of parishioners whose congregations are facing a similar reality. "Empty Houses" is a resource that can help people and congregations prepare for a difficult journey through potentially unstable times.

Outdoor leadership expert John Graham writes that one of the most important things about leading people through the wilderness is preparation. One of the ways we prepare for this kind of trip is by ensuring that we have the necessary supplies and resources available for the journey. We will have to provide enough food and water for scheduled mealtimes and breaks. We also have to provide for any emergencies we experience along the trail.[2]

One of the things we also need when we prepare for a journey is a map. A map will be helpful in our congregations as well. When we discuss the church as it moves into the twenty-first century we often use the metaphor of the wilderness. We speak of individuals and communities making their way through the deserts and forests in an effort to find a new place where they can live out their faith and response to God's invitation to love and service. Any wilderness journey requires planning. This is especially true when we find ourselves in the desert. Anyone traveling through the desert has to know where the places are in which they can find water and other resources. We have to know where we can rest in safety. We have to know where the roads are and how we can find our way to the agreed upon destination.

Hiking through the woods can be an interesting, inspiring and energizing experience. Traveling through the wilderness can also be a confusing and frightening time. We want to turn back and return to the familiar places and routines of our everyday lives. We wonder why this particular journey is necessary in the first place. This confusion and fear becomes all too real if we get lost and cannot find our way to where we are going. Being a part of a Christian congregation making its way into the twenty-first century can have its moments of inspiration and it can also be unsettling. There are times when we enjoy the surroundings of a meadow and there are also times when we find ourselves in a desert or on a battlefield.

"Empty Houses" can be used as a resource for people in a congregation traveling through the wilderness of transition and choice. "Empty Houses" can also be used as a road map helping people find a way towards a renewed future for both themselves and those with whom they share a congregation. This future may be unclear. There may be some uncertainty around whether or not there are problems that affect the overall viability of the congregation. It's often difficult to know these things. It can be difficult to take a break from the business of community life to confront some of the larger questions and challenges facing the congregation. Not everyone will be on the same page when it comes to awareness around the problems and challenges facing the congregation.

If you are not sure whether or not your congregation is facing serious viability issues try naming which of the following apply to what is happening. This isn't a scientific survey but it can raise some important issues and questions for further discussion.

• Has the attendance declined?

- Has the average age of your congregation increased?
- Has there been a noticeable change in the level of givings and overall financial state of the congregation?
- Are there any maintenance jobs that have been postponed because the financial and human resources are not available to complete them?
- Has the local community changed and how has this affected the congregation?

If two or three of these points apply to your congregation then you and the people sharing the pews of your congregation have to talk about what is happening. You don't have to discuss every little thing that is perceived as being "wrong" with your congregation. Perhaps the important place to begin is with the major issues. As Thomas Kuhn once wrote in a work on paradigm shifts, "The scientist who pauses to examine every anomaly he notes will seldom get significant work done."[3]

"Empty Houses" is a resource that addresses the challenge of assessing the viability of a congregation. There are two major possibilities offered for this assessment. There is the simple way in which people simply review the numbers and reflect on the present situation. There is the more complicated process of actually creating a plan and testing the situation and interpreting the results so that a decision can be made. So much depends on the time and resources available to the congregation for the diagnostic effort. "Empty Houses" can help a congregation build a plan by which they gather results to facilitate the decision around closure. I point to resources that can help a congregation discover what it needs to bring about change and renewal. "Empty Houses" also helps address issues and questions around decisions, planning and pastoral care. It outlines some of the potential realities and challenges of grief and conflict. "Empty Houses" provides some comment on worship possibilities and hopes for new opportunities.

Christians are an Easter people fluent in the language of death and resurrection. Every spring we address the reality of Christ's death and the celebration of his resurrection. We can address the presence of death and resurrection in our individual lives and we can also deal with these realities as they apply to our congregations.

"Empty Houses" is a resource for congregations facing life and death issues. It is for those congregations facing the challenging and difficult work of closure. It has also been my intention that "Empty Houses" begin a deeper and more extended discussion around church closures and redevelopment as many of our communities face increasing challenges while they move into the future. Let's face it— closing churches is not something we want to talk about. It's not something we want to do. It's a conversation we cannot ignore, however. In the time I have been serving United Church of Canada congregations here in the Calgary area eight congregations from our denomination have closed. In this same period of time only two have been created. Five of the eight congregations that have closed have been involved in mergers while the rest have seen their membership dispersed to other congregations.

In October of 2004 the local Anglican diocese unexpectedly announced the closure of three parishes.[4] Similar situations are being experienced across North America. The Roman Catholic Archdiocese of Boston, for example, has been dealing with the closure of roughly eighty parishes. Many other denominations are facing choices that are going to affect hundreds of communities in both urban and rural areas.

Why do churches close? Perhaps this is one of the fundamental questions we can ask as we consider the work ahead. There may be some who try to avoid this question. We talk about growth, change and redevelopment. We hold up the senior pastors of mega-churches as we would the all stars of our professional sports teams. We don't want to talk about anything negative. We don't want to talk about anything that may suggest failure on the part of lay people and clergy leaders. However, it is important we talk about the difficult issues and realities. It's important we talk about those situations in which we need to consider some difficult questions and possibilities. We are not helping anyone when we avoid the conversations that promise only hard work and potential conflict with friends and family. These don't always have to be difficult conversations necessarily.

There is information that may be helpful as a congregation reaches the point of having to make important decisions. Churches close for any number of reasons. There may be financial challenges that can no longer be ignored. Parishioners may be unwilling or unable to explore new worship styles that could reach people in their communities. The United Brethren denomination in the United States identifies four reasons for closing a church: [5] "a) The church is weak in such areas as membership, attendance, finances and purpose, b) There is a desire to merge with another congregation, c) The congregation is unable to carry out a meaningful ministry, d) The congregation consists of less than 10 resident families." If there is a concern about any of these areas then their conference can intervene. If average attendance, for example, falls below 50 people on a Sunday over a two-year period then conference can begin trying to find out what is happening.

When we talk about numbers and requirements there is one thing we can keep in mind as we go about our work in the church. Every situation is different and has to be dealt with accordingly. We have to focus on each congregation as an individual entity. As previously discussed, there could be changes happening in the community that call for a change in how the ministry develops. A congregation could be moving away from a vision or style of ministry. There can be dynamics within the congregation preventing newcomers from returning and finding a place within a given congregation. It could be any one of these reasons or it could be all of them. Each congregation is unique and every situation is different. This is what makes a decision to close so challenging. This is why planning a time for the closure is also difficult.

So we can bring our individual experiences, questions and challenges to the work of looking ahead to the future of our congregations. We can bring our skills and experiences to the work of making our way to the new beginnings as promised in the Gospel and that we have committed ourselves to living out. My hope is that "Empty Houses" can have a place in this work of bringing about new life in God's community.

***

In writing "Empty Houses" I have had to make some decisions concerning the material I have both included and left out. Throughout this work I have tried to abide by the Younger Pliny's wisdom when he writes, "I think a writer's first duty is to read his title, to keep on asking himself what he set out to say, and to realize that he will not say too much if he sticks to his theme, though he certainly will if he brings in extraneous material". [6] I hope that I have kept the "extraneous material" to a minimum. A number of people have helped keep me focused on the important issues and I would like to take this opportunity to thank them for everything they have offered.

I would like to thank the people who have brought "Empty Houses" to life. I would like to thank my primary proof-readers Judi Crawford-Parr, Wilbert MacLennan, The Rev. Dr. Douglas Cowan, Noelle Allen and Jason Allen. The Rev. David Brewer has provided the artwork for the cover and I am grateful for his generosity. I would like to thank Professors Irving Hexham, PhD, Henry Srebrnik, PhD, and the rest of the Friday afternoon coffee klatch for their encouragement, advice and wisdom. Shona Welsh and Will Black have both provided advice and coaching that have been helpful. Natalie Fuhr, at Booksurge, has been a real help in bringing this book to print. I would also like to thank Alan and Marlene Faint for the times they helped with computer crises and important conversations over lunch.

I would especially like to thank my spouse Trish for her love, patience and support throughout the writing of "Empty Houses". Family and friends have all made important contributions to this project. And Rosie! I can't forget the "Best Little Dog in the Whole World".

Endnotes

1. Camus, Albert "On Jules Roy's 'La Vallee Heureuse'". L'Arche, February 1947
2. Graham, John "Outdoor Leadership: Technique, Common Sense and Self-Confidence" (Seattle, 2003 Ed.), P.23
3. Kuhn, Thomas "The Structure of Scientific Revolutions" (Chicago, 1962, 1970), P.82
4. Woodard, Joe "City's Anglican Churches Caught In Global Turmoil" in October 30th, 2004 Calgary Herald
5. United Brethren Discipline 2001-2005
6. Pliny, "The Letters of the Younger Pliny" Translated by Betty Radice (London, 1969), P. 144

Chapter One
Diagnosis

It frequently happens when we visit the doctor. We schedule a visit to solve a problem. Sometimes the doctor makes an immediate diagnosis based on something obvious like a limp. The doctor may be able to identify a problem by looking at a mark or something else out of the ordinary. In many other cases though, it takes considerable testing to reach a valid diagnosis. The doctor may want to see the results from a blood test or X-ray or run a stress test or arrange for a CAT scan.

A congregation can be viewed in a similar way. There may be obvious signs that there are problems. These signs may be strong enough that our course of action is plainly laid out for us. Financial and attendance figures, for example, may have changed to the point where we need to take action without testing or diagnosis. A group of people may gather for an annual meeting and see the necessary course of action based on the information they receive. We may have a feeling, however, that all is not well but the root cause may not be all that easy to identify. Like the doctor, testing is required.

There are many examples of potential problems

congregations face on a regular basis. One example of a problem that can affect the congregation's viability is attendance. We may notice a drop in the average Sunday attendance and ask what's going on. We can ask people why they have stopped attending worship. We can ask people in the nearby community why they choose other activities on Sunday morning. We can create surveys that help give us the kind of information we need in order to make important and necessary decisions.

Using this language of testing and diagnosis allows us to compare a congregation to a living organism.[1] There are many times in which The Bible refers to this notion of the body of Christ. In First Corinthians we read: "For just as the body is one and has many members, and all of the body, though many, are one body, so it is with Christ" (1 Cor. 12: 12). Just as the systems of the body have to work well together to be healthy, the different parts of a congregation need to work well with one another. When some part of the body has a problem, we have a problem. A congregation cannot continue to function when some of its parts are failing. In both cases, long-term viability is threatened and intervention is required to avoid a crisis.

As any living being, the congregation has a life span. It is a life span that Gary McIntosh talks about when he writes, "When church growth is charted many churches show typical patterns of growth, plateau and decline."[2] This is a natural part of life. The writer of Ecclesiastes mentions the time and place for "every matter under heaven". This includes a "time to be born and a time to die". (3:2) McIntosh explains, "the first fifteen to twenty years of a church's life are typically its most dynamic ones."[3] Congregations normally experience a plateau after about forty years.

Congregations plateau, and decline for a variety of reasons. Its members may lose touch with the original vision. They may become comfortable with the community dynamics of the congregation. We make friends and build relationships when we become a part of a community of faith. As a congregation grows and changes are required, we may experience the temptation to try to keep things the way they were. This may result in members leaving as well as failure to attract new members.

One of the ways in which a plateau becomes a decline is if exhaustion sets in through lack of growth. People within the congregation may remain in their jobs until they simply burn out. Whether from force of habit or a particular need to hold on to a position of power within the congregation, the same people do the same thing year after year and new people are not encouraged to become involved.

McIntosh writes, "if nothing is done to change the trend a church eventually disintegrates into a period of stagnation and decline over the next twenty or more years.... When a congregation is in decline volunteers are difficult to find and members say 'it's the staff's job. That's what we pay them to do' "[4] "Stagnation" is an important word here. When a pool of water remains unchanged it becomes polluted and poisonous. Water remains fresh if it keeps moving and flowing. The challenge is to maintain a healthy flow of energy and ideas so the congregation can grow and thrive.

Some congregations plateau and decline due to external forces beyond the control of its members. There may be changes in neighborhood demographics. People tend to move around as their life situation changes, moving in and out of communities in an effort to find work or housing that is suitable for the age and stage of their family. A congregation may be in a town with only one source of employment, for example. If this source of employment closes or moves away then the people will move with the company or pursue other employment opportunities. When people find new communities they may also find a new church.

There may be challenges unique to particular denominations. The North American Roman Catholic Church, for example, has experienced a reduction in the number of priests. In the Archdiocese of Boston there were 1,197 priests in 1984. By 2003, that number shrank to 887. This is one local example of a widespread situation affecting the ability of Catholic Church leaders to find ordained leadership for the roughly nineteen thousand parishes in the United States.[5]

Another recent challenge has been to find the funds for court decisions calling for the payment of increasingly large legal settlements to various claimants.[6] This includes both sexual abuse cases and residential school claims. This pressure will continue to increase, as many of these claims have not yet been settled.

This Chapter identifies the question "Does your congregation have problems?" and provides a high level overview of how to determine whether or not a problem exists. It outlines how the book will provide assistance in problem recognition and diagnosis. How do we know if there's a problem that will affect how we live out God's call in the long term? The following is a brief list of challenges that may be affecting your congregation. Take a moment and identify which ones apply to your congregation. If you can think of any other questions that can be asked, please feel free to add them.[7]

- Does your congregation have a clear vision that can be articulated on a t-shirt or bumper sticker?
- Has the attendance declined?
- Has the average age of your congregation increased?
- Has there been a noticeable change in the level of givings and overall financial state of the congregation?
- Is there an organized effort to reach out to people in the community who have little or no church connection?
- Are you having trouble finding people to fill certain jobs in the congregation's organizational structure?
- When was the last time a newcomer took on a major role in the congregation?

- Are there any maintenance jobs that have been postponed because the financial and human resources are not available to complete them?
- Is your church a safe place where people can come and feel welcome?
- Does the congregation have regular social events to help build community?
- Has the local community changed and how has this affected the congregation?

If four or five of these challenges apply to your congregation then more investigation is necessary. Where to begin? Reviewing previous annual reports to research information that may identify some trends is a good place to start. Pay particular attention to any financial reports that identify trends that affect the long-term viability of your congregation. Look carefully at the expense column in the financial statements in these annual reports. One of the underrated reasons for any increase in expenses is inflation. One group has used the expression "Budget creep" to explain this.[8] Congregations with a stable membership experience budget creep when inflation pushes prices up while givings remain unchanged. And in smaller congregations even the slightest change in the financial picture can drastically affect overall viability.

Review attendance figures and frequency of services such as weddings, baptisms, and funerals, which will give some indication of how active the congregation is and its involvement in the life of the neighboring community. These numbers are an important indicator of the health of the congregation. Some denominations, for example, have established criteria around average attendance. If attendance falls below a certain level, the situation requires an in-depth examination.

The Roman Catholic Archdiocese of Boston uses a type of numerical formula as a way of helping it assess the viability of a congregation. This formula is called the "sacramental index" and it involves the number of funerals, baptisms and weddings celebrated at the individual church. If the "magic number", so to speak, is below a certain level then the parish will be considered for "consolidation". "Consolidation" is often a word used when mergers and closures are planned. This is not the only indicator. We can also consider worship attendance and the physical state of parish buildings.[9] Buildings in need of extensive repair can be a real drain on the financial and human resources of both the congregation and denomination.

When there is some question about the long-term health of a congregation it is time to seriously consider a change and transformation plan. This plan should incorporate the questions already noted as well as include items that are raised both by individuals in the congregation or by people connected with the wider denomination. Denominations owning property, for example, will have a stake in what happens in a given congregation. With this kind of interest in the congregation a denomination may want a voice in the creation of any transformation plan.

The participants will vary from congregation to congregation; however, success in all cases depends on an inclusive process that gives the congregation a clear understanding of the issues and the alternatives it has to embrace for successful change.

One of my previous congregations had a plan that called for growth in areas like congregational membership and programming. It called for facility upgrades and even the sale of a neighboring property to help provide the necessary financial resources to help fund the work of the congregation while it was living out this plan. This plan was developed in the hope of bringing about change and growth in the congregation and was a positive response that faced up to problems that could lead to closure.

A good transformation plan needs many things. It must

call for a renewed congregational vision. It must consider important things like finances, innovation and outreach. It must also identify a decision point in the process. A decision point is similar to a fork in the road in which a person must decide on which path to take. Some examples for a congregation are the decision to merge with another congregation, the decision to make a major capital and maintenance investment, the decision to sell the church building and rent a smaller location.

One of the first important steps in the planning process is called "discernment". "Discernment" is simply showing insight and understanding. From a Christian perspective this can mean having some insight into God's will for us. This can also mean the work of coming to some understanding of what this insight means for us.

When a person feels that God is calling them to a particular ministry, for example, they may begin a period of considering this call and seeing if this is, indeed, what God is calling them to do. They are figuring out if this is a part of God's plan for their lives. When a person is experiencing a time of discernment we can encourage them to pray and to reflect. We can also encourage a person to consider the cost and implications of what they are looking into. Will a person have to move away in response to this call? Will s/he have to leave a job or pursue more education? The Bible contains many stories of people who had made tremendous sacrifices in responding to God's call. Individual people can discern what God is calling them to do. Congregations may also experience a need to enter some sort of collective discernment process.

Discernment requires asking questions. One important thing to keep in mind is that if we ask a question, we also need to be open to the response. We may not always agree with the answers we receive. We may not even like these responses. Do we really want to know the answer to questions concerning the viability of our congregations and the future of our ministries? Asking hard questions is not a pleasant process; however, life teaches us that doing nothing is also a decision and one that often takes us to places we would not actively chose.

For me, one of the most important questions a discerning congregation can ask is found in the Alban Institute publication entitled "Ending With Hope". In this resource Keith Spencer asks the question, "What is God calling us to do in this place?"[10] The answer to this question helps contribute to the development of a vision.

One of the early leaders of Great Britain's Royal Flying Corps was Hugh Trenchard. Trenchard was an important part of the development of this Corps during the First World War. He helped build the squadrons necessary to support the troops in the field. This was the beginning of a long and distinguished career that eventually led to his becoming an "Air Marshall". In describing Trenchard's character and leadership style one person has said that he possessed "a clear sense of direction".[11]

A vision is just that, a "clear sense of direction." And it is critical that renewing congregations develop a clear vision or sense of direction. There are two questions that are helpful in the process of developing a vision: What is the congregation supposed to be doing and to whom are we supposed to be ministering? In finding a new vision some congregations will focus on a particular community or section of a city. Some may focus on a particular task. Other congregations may choose to focus on a certain age group. Some congregations will focus on ministering to certain ethnic communities. In helping a congregation live out this renewed vision a congregation may choose a style of music and worship that suits their new direction.

In trying to put this new vision into words it is important to focus on a statement that is both clear and concise. A vision is something that can be shared with someone over coffee or be printed on a T-shirt. One example that comes to mind is "Spread the Gospel—That's it—that's all." This brief statement provides a beginning point from which a series of value statements, goals and tasks can be developed.

How can a congregation build a new vision? This may happen as the congregation makes its way through the work of studying the community around them. There may be changes in demographics that point to new possibilities. There may be issues and problems that can be addressed. Meetings may be useful to help planners check in and see what kind of information is coming in. What does this information say and where are the opportunities for change and growth?

One thing that should be remembered throughout this discernment and visioning process is that we can be easily distracted from our task. Martin Marty writes, "The externals can easily lead (the congregation) into avoiding the basic questions of mission and purpose."[12] These questions around mission and vision have to come first and be held before the congregation at every point in the renewal and decision process. They help keep us focused and contribute to the work of setting goals and priorities.

In considering God's call for a given congregation we should focus attention on building the community that will be needed to live out this call. Developing a strong and vibrant community life is important to any congregation. It is important that congregations build strong attachments that help bring people together and also that it builds a vision that can offer direction for this growing community. David Kuhl has written, "Without attachment, one feels abandoned.... One longs to belong, to be attached, to be a part of the family, group or community.... It is a matter of survival as well as emotional development."[13]

In talking about building "strong attachments" I have some thoughts about "openness" and "inclusivity". While we can share a warm and intimate fellowship as a congregation, we can fall away from the ongoing challenge of welcoming

new people into our faith communities. One of the ways we
share the good news is by inviting people to gather with us to
share in worship and the ongoing life of the congregation.
I had a revealing conversation with a local pastor a number
of years ago. We were discussing the change and growth
happening in his congregation. When we were discussing
the welcoming of new people this pastor quickly came to the
one concept his congregation tried to practice at all times.
This one concept was: It ministers to the people who come
through their doors. This may seem simple enough, but it
also contains its share of challenges.

One important way of building this kind of inviting and
inclusive community is the development of small group
ministries. These small groups of between eight and ten
people meet on a regular basis to share in prayer and Bible
Study. They touch base on issues that are important to them
and discuss recent events that have an impact on their lives.
And for congregations that find finances a challenge small
groups are relatively inexpensive.

In discussing this need to build the kind of community
that creates and nourishes relationships, we can also have a
look at a community that builds both its spiritual life and its
relationship with God. Gary McIntosh asks "How can we work
with God in building a faithful church?"[14] How can we build
a church, or congregation, that listens for the Gospel, works
at understanding its message, and shares this good news with
people in the surrounding community?

All of this talk about small groups and community
building is pointless if we do not face other important
questions. One of these questions is whether or not the
congregation has the resources to finance a given plan. Some
congregations have let a deteriorating situation go for so long
that the decision has been made for them. I remember a news
story from a couple of years ago where an airplane ran out of
fuel while over the Atlantic Ocean. I'm not sure if there was
a fuel leak or someone merely filled the tank with less fuel

than was needed for the ocean crossing. The bottom line is that the plane ran out of fuel and had to make an emergency landing with no power. With so many people on board the pilot had no other choice but to land the plane as safely as possible. He made some quick calculations and brought the plane down, as someone would land a glider. As any pilot will tell you this is the most dangerous way to land a plane. How many congregations find themselves in this situation? How many congregations wait until the energy and money runs out before being forced into the situation where they have to close their doors?

Congregations in this position keep hoping for those visitors to come through the door. They wait for that huge donation to come in the mail. They keep praying for that huge demographic shift that has been predicted for their area. The planning process must begin when concerns about the health of the congregation are first being raised. K. Spencer writes, "...too many congregations put off conversations about viability until there are no longer choices to be made."[15] Aubrey Malphurs has said this another way when he writes, "It's easier to have babies than raise the dead!"[16]

I would suggest that planning and decision-making are far more effective when there are resources available to help examine the possibilities of renewing a congregation or providing time for a dignified closure. A congregation facing financial problems can ask some serious questions about how resources can be made available to see a plan and transition process through to the planned decision point. Is there property that can be sold? Are there grants and loans available from the denomination? When it comes to financial resources beyond the congregation, I would urge caution when considering such possibilities as a bank loan. While interest rates may be favourable they remain an added burden to be built in to the budget. Options around financing this plan can be discussed by consulting with people from the wider church.

Decisions concerning the future of the congregation, and whether or not to begin a renewal process must be honoured and supported by the wider church. The wider church, as we have already mentioned, can share in this planning process. The wider church also must hold the congregation to this decision. Martin Marty writes, "Every move a local congregation makes must be made in light of its smaller part in the whole church in the world."[17] This "whole church" Marty refers to can be the denomination in which the congregation is a part. The "whole church" can be the collection of congregations within a given geographical area. For our purposes here, I think that it is important that we concentrate on the relationship between the congregation and its respective denomination. I think it's also important to consider the work of the church within the geographical area of the given congregation.

What must happen to bring about a renewed congregation? What will it take to reverse the decline of the congregation in question? This is an important question for many reasons. As we will see in the Chapter Two there are decisions that will need to be made at the congregational level, and there will be decisions required within the different levels of the wider church.

Leadership is always an important topic during change. Who is leading this effort to test the health of a congregation and help make a diagnosis? Many would suggest that it is the minister's role to lead the investigation and come up with a plan. One of the potential roles for the clergy person in this planning process could be as shepherd and guide to the people in the congregation. The clergy person may also need to function as a coach and coordinator. Communication is an important part of this job as well. Effective communication requires accurate information. This places the clergy person in the position of being one of the primary resource people available to the congregation. This is especially important when we consider the relationship that tends to develop between the congregation and the denomination in which they are a part.

Others may turn to the group in the congregation having organizational and management responsibilities (Referred to here as "the Board"). This Board can work with both the minister and the wider church in creating and evaluating whatever transition plan emerges from this planning process. The collective group can gather whatever information they need to help build the plan.[18]

The Board will have a critical leadership role in this planning and transition process. It should have a good idea of the needs of the congregation, and be prepared to offer advice on these needs. It can be a sounding board for the minister and staff as well as one of the main contact points between the congregation and the wider church.

Both clergy and lay people have an important leadership role in the congregation. This leadership can be shown in the planning process and it can also be seen in other places. Speed Leas writes, "What has made the great leaders of the world notable is not the absence of conflict or struggle from the implementation of their leadership—just the opposite—greatness has come from the way they addressed adversity."[19] When we want to show leadership we may need to ruffle a few feathers and deal with the conflict and then, move on to complete our task and accomplish our goals. Trying to keep everyone happy is not realistic. Chapter Five on conflict will deal with this in more detail.

There is a Bach cantata that begins with, "Sheep may safely graze where a good shepherd is watching." "Good Shepherds", so to speak, can help people share in the challenges ahead. "Good shepherds" can help provide effective leadership for a community that may or may not have any idea of where it has to go. "Good Shepherds" can listen and ask questions. They can also offer care and support that can help contribute to the effective leadership of the congregation. Effective leadership from both the clergy and lay people can help offer both the guidance and protection necessary to negotiate the difficult path of church transition, renewal or closure.

It is important to clarify the roles, and authority of everyone involved in the planning process up front. Many church people seem leery of "authority". Throughout the history of the church there have been too many cases where authority has been abused, which I believe has resulted in contemporary congregations shying away from the concept altogether. Authority remains, however, an important aspect of a congregation's leadership. Kenneth Haugk writes, "Authority in and of itself is a neutral term....the proper, timely use of authority is good and serves as a strong preventative measure against the development of antagonism."[20] While authority can be abused it can also be helpful. Congregational leaders must learn how to use authority in healthy and appropriate ways.

One of the things that makes this use of authority difficult is the natural human need to be liked. Haugk writes, "Physicians do not usually give prescriptions to their patients based on which medicine tastes best, but according to what is best for the patient's health and well being."[21] In the midst of a crisis people want and need effective leadership. Whether they like the person or not becomes irrelevant. People want, and need skilled leaders. In becoming effective leaders, we cannot be limited by the need to be universally liked. People need skills and talents rather than popularity to help get them through a difficult planning process. A congregation navigating this challenging process needs a skilled leader. Change and transition are not always for the faint of heart and innovation demands a lot of openness and hard work from anyone involved in this process.

How can change be introduced in a congregation? This is the question that we cannot ignore or run away from. There is an ancient saying that we can't step into the same river twice. It speaks to the constant flow of time and our inability to affect or change this reality. There are realities and changes in life that are beyond our control. We can gripe and complain all we want but that doesn't do much to alter the situation. The main thing is that we deal constructively with these things as they arise.

Peter Drucker writes, "The enterprise that does not innovate inevitably ages and declines. And in a period of rapid change such as the present, an entrepreneurial period, the decline will be fast."[22] If we visit a dentist do we want them using nineteenth century technology? We accept and tolerate change in so many other places in our lives and yet we seem to find it difficult when it happens in our faith communities.

Abraham Heschel has written, "Views, just as leaves, are bound to wither, because the world is in flux. But so many of us would rather be faithful to outworn views than to undergo the strain of re-examination and revision."[23] These words can apply to more than simply belief. We can apply these words to things like music and worship style, and to the way in which we reach out to community. The one constant that may exist in the church is that the status quo is not an option. In 1939, the German army invaded Poland and attacked with the latest planes, tanks and tactics. The Polish army came out to meet them with horses and lances. The results were all too predictable.

Perhaps we need to encourage people to see change in another perspective. Colin Murray-Parkes writes, "Times of transition are times of opportunity and any confrontation with an unfamiliar world is both an opportunity for autonomous mastery and a threat to one's adjustment to life."[24]

When we discuss innovation we must be careful about the kinds of changes that we make. Not all changes are positive and life giving. Not all changes will be in keeping with what we are about as a church or necessarily lead to any kind of progress. Change must be appropriate. William Bridges has written that changes need to be a part of a "larger and beneficial pattern."[25]

Transitions bring about endings as well as new beginnings.

Bridges writes, "Every transition begins with an ending...We have to let go of the old thing before we pick up the new."[26] Bridges' statement can lead us to ask another important question. We can ask ourselves if we really want to change. Do we really want to let go of everything that we have come to know and find comfort in? Do we really want to leave the familiar to face something new and unfamiliar?

Changes can cause chaos and uncertainty. They can remind us of everything that is happening in life and can be an overwhelming experience. A person can all too easily lose his/ her bearings, and become disoriented. I remember taking a drive a couple of years ago. Snow was covering the ground. It was late in the afternoon in winter and the sky was getting dark. There was a point in the trip when I could no longer tell the difference between the snow cover and sky. Finding the horizon became difficult and disorienting.

The kinds of change that our congregations consider will need to be tested. Paul once made the suggestion that we need to test everything in an effort to find out what is good (1 Thessalonians 5:21) "Examine yourselves to see if you are living in the faith. Test Yourselves." (2 Corinthians 13:5) This is a continuing part of the discernment process.

One thing that cannot be ignored is the spiritual dimension of the congregation's collective and individual lives. In a recent article Gordon Harland writes that we need to consider the ongoing spiritual quest going on in society today.[27] How do we tap into this quest? How do we interpret the divine to people struggling through their day-to-day lives? People are asking a lot of questions. Many of these questions can be dealt with but others are beyond our understanding. Confronting these questions is necessary for long-term viability.

How can a congregation develop a vision and ministry that speaks to people? How can it find out whether or not it has been successful? Harland writes, "surely the major task of the church today is to appropriate, articulate and make available this framework of meaning for a restless, searching culture."[28] Harland goes on to suggest "Translating the gospel into a new culture is risky." This work involves many aspects of a congregation's life.

One of the challenges is in the area of worship and music. Worship and music are two important ways of translating the Gospel for a culture that may not be as knowledgeable about the church, or its message, as it once was. Worship is an important, if not the most central aspect of any congregation's life. It is central to both growing and declining congregations. Carl Dudley writes, "Worship is not withdrawal from the world, but an affirmation of God in the midst".[29] It can be the recognition that God is present with the congregation as it makes its way through discernment and the planning process that can follow. "He's Got the Whole World in His Hands" was an important song in its time and place. What are the songs that speak to us? What is the music that helps us make the connection between human and divine? This is one of the main reasons why music and worship leaders must have a place in which they can participate in whatever plan is developed.

Perhaps a part of this plan can be the study of new forms of music. A workshop can be held in which people listen to new music and offer their thoughts on whether or not it could be used in worship. This workshop can be scheduled for a time that is different from the regular worship service. Any new music to be introduced to the congregation can be done so through choral presentations and specially scheduled hymn sings.

Whenever we examine the worship program of a congregation we can ask one important question. Are we communicating the Gospel or are we simply entertaining people?[30] Are we providing effective ministry or are we doing a song and dance in an effort to boost the numbers of people in worship? There is no easy answer to these questions. This is where vision becomes so important. The vision becomes a guiding principal for everyone involved in planning and leading the congregation's worship program. It can be a principal that helps the entire congregation examine the surrounding communities in an effort to find out what must be done to reach out to people.

As we consider the relationship between the congregation and its surrounding culture, we can also reconsider the congregation's current location and building. This is another important part of any change and growth plan. Location and real estate can have a huge impact on the health of a congregation. A recent article in the New Brunswick Reader notes how the condition of the building can become a crushing responsibility for a dwindling congregation.[31]

My previous congregation, for example, was housed in a large brick structure. As this building aged the maintenance needs and challenges increased. These increasing demands were difficult for a small congregation to manage and pay for. So much money and energy went into the building that there wasn't much left for ministry. People worked hard but one can only imagine what could have developed had the congregation been free to pursue other goals.

The one issue at my previous congregation that told us that something was not going according to plan was the windows. We were told that the windows needed to be painted and repaired or we would be facing a tremendous bill for their repair or eventual replacement. Repair estimates were obtained and brought forward to the Board. The Board made the decision that the congregation could not afford needed repair, as money wasn't there. This seemingly minor decision raised some important questions. Perhaps the most important one concerned the congregation's ability to meet the financial goals outlined in their transition plan. If the congregation couldn't afford to make routine and critical repairs then how would it ensure the long-range viability of a community meeting in that place?

Ian Black makes the observation that "The work of the

church has at its root the "ekklesia", the gathering of the people of God."[32] The people of God can gather and worship in buildings. They can also worship in other places. Some of the early Christian communities met in caves and open fields. The main thing is that we can learn from the use of these varied locations so that we focus our energies on ministry, and not bricks and mortar. Place is important but our relationship with God is more important.

Ian Black reminds us "One of the Ten Commandments is against idolatry".[33] From a Christian perspective, idolatry is an effort to replace God with a thing or a person. In this case I would suggest that individuals within a congregation worship the building instead of God. It is not always something that is done intentionally. People invest a lot of time and energy into their church buildings. It should not surprise us that this investment translates into a sense of ownership. This ownership can be one of the things that influence our decision-making concerning the church building. This concept of idolatry in a congregation can also be applied to a program, particular style of worship and so on. The important question that can be raised any number of times concerns the object of our worship. Are we worshipping God or something else? This question must not be lost as the planning and assessment process proceeds.

In discussing our feelings and attitudes about the church building I am reminded of something a person once told me about her office. She worked in a young company that had moved four times in six years. These moves were made because of the changing needs and nature of the work of the company. As the company changed, the property needs changed accordingly. Our congregations can also consider this kind of mobility. The bottom line is that we cannot afford any kind of obsessive loyalty to a building. As we have said before, a building is important but it should not replace God.

The barriers to reconsidering the building and location

of a congregation are the level of emotional attachment we develop to these buildings. This attachment seems to prevent us from examining the possibilities of moving to another location. This attachment can also cloud our judgment and help us miss opportunities for growth and viability elsewhere. One church leader sums it up, "All of this investment in buildings is crippling our ministry."[34]

So many resources have been going into bricks and mortar that staffing levels and programming are being affected. Many congregations, for example, are postponing important staffing and ministry decisions because they simply cannot afford them. In referring to one Canadian archdiocese, Solange Desantis writes, "Maintaining … buildings has forced them to eliminate curacies, cut their support of diocesan mission budget, reduce staff and draw on capital reserves."[35] This limits a congregation's ability to live out its vision and properly resource the people trying to carry out important volunteer work in both the congregation and community itself. We'll be talking more about issues surrounding the church building, and how it affects ministry, in Chapter Three.

In discussing the possibility of relocating, church consultant Lyle Schaller suggests that one option for a declining congregation is to relocate.[36] Given the changes happening in many of our communities it may become important to find a more central location as people move about. It may also become important to find a smaller or more functional building.

Hopefully, building and location are the jumping off points to wider reflection. How can we look beyond the bricks and mortar housing our congregation? "What does a healthy, viable church really look like?" How do we find renewal as a congregation? What do we need to do to achieve this renewal? How will this renewal affect our work and identity as a congregation?

These are issues and questions based on something that

Terry Anderson asks when he writes, "What is the nature of a truly human life?"[37] We can broaden this question to ask about the nature of a truly human congregation. It is here that we confront the need to discuss quality and quantity. Any transition plan needs to balance these two. Churches tend to pay a lot of attention to numbers. With all of these so called "Mega churches" in the spot light we may find ourselves looking inward to see if we match up. We find ourselves making comparisons based on what we see as their "success".

I am not sure that an exclusive focus on quotas, and tracking numbers is a wise idea when assessing the viability of a congregation. These kinds of numbers can be helpful but numbers alone do not tell the complete story. I have seen some rural congregations survive with around thirty people in their pews. So much depends on expenses and building needs. Thirty people worshipping in a large, and aging, brick building will be challenged; thirty people in a smaller newer facility will likely not.

We must identify ways to measure the success of our plan. In a game of any sort we measure the progress of a team by simply checking out the scoreboard. A congregation will need to develop a yard stick by which progress can be measured. One plan called for a ten percent annual increase in membership. Another congregation set a goal in which a significant percentage of their confirmed membership would be active in small group ministries. These are things that can be noted and measured in an effort to help in measuring the congregation's viability.

Do not place too much faith in numbers though. Eric Swanson suggests that we need to change our focus from achieving success to finding "significance".[38] Swanson goes on to say, "Not all churches are destined to be great. But regardless of size, they can go about doing good."[39] We must try to figure out how a given congregation can achieve this "significance". What will bring about a ministry containing both quality and quantity?

One of the ways that we can build a quality congregation is by having a look at possible programs that reach out to people and bring them into the congregation's worship and community life. Swanson outlines the experience of a literacy program at Hope Presbyterian in Memphis, Tennessee. It's a simple effort where kids are offered the chance to improve their literacy skills. When young people learn to read their prospects increase and they can look forward to a more hopeful future.[40]

Peter Drucker addresses quality from a business perspective when he writes, "Customers pay for what is of use to them and gives them value. Nothing else constitutes quality."[41] We can play the most beautiful music around but if it doesn't touch people then it is not going to help us.

"Quality" can be applied to many aspects of the ethical issues related to death and dying. This is an important consideration when we are trying to determine an individual's "quality of life".[42] "Quality of life" can mean different things to different people. Will a particular treatment, for example, lead to a level of impairment preventing a person from living a fulfilling and meaningful life? I think there is an opportunity to raise a similar question when it comes to the health and viability of a congregation. We have an opportunity to ask some questions around the present life of a congregation and the things that are necessary to renew and rejuvenate the community of faith.

A good plan needs a lot of preparation and study. Who is the plan targeting? Where is the community that the congregation is reaching out to? What is the culture? What will it take to gain a response?

A plan that encompasses things such as quality and quantity must be firm and also flexible at the same time. When we begin the examination of a community we may be surprised by what we find. We may study the local demographics, for example, and discover needs and opportunities that have not been identified or considered in any previous planning or outreach efforts. Have there been changes in the average income of people in a neighborhood? Have there been any changes in the employment picture?

As I am writing this I notice a news item in which a large employer is closing a factory and laying off over 1400 people. I wonder how this closure will affect the community in which this factory had operated. I wonder how this closure will affect the area churches. What can the churches do in helping the affected people deal with this loss? Programs and ministries addressing this kind of change and transition can be added. Small groups can be developed in which people can share their emotions and feelings and help each other cope with the uncertainty and instability. As the population of the area changes, there may also be a need to cancel any programs no longer necessary to the life of these congregations.

In one of my previous congregations we were seeing major changes in the neighborhood. Many of the older residents were selling their homes. Younger people were moving in and beginning to participate in the area's community life. The congregation I was serving noticed these changes and began anticipating how these would affect us. The one thing that we assumed was that these younger folks coming into the neighborhood would have families. Many of these newer families did have children but, surprisingly, a significant number did not, and it was one of the facts that affected our plans.

A plan for assessing the viability of a congregation must include responses to any unexpected findings. The plan needs to allow for the pursuit of any opportunities uncovered by an effort to find out more about a congregation's surroundings and the people who populate these surroundings. God may call us to make significant changes in response to the direction in which our community is moving.

One of the final things that a congregation may need to consider in the plan is the structure by which the life and work of the worshipping community are organized and managed. As congregations change, the way that they are managed may require change as well. Will a Board of six people, for example, be able to provide oversight of a congregation growing beyond an average attendance of one hundred and fifty people? Will a congregation need a "circle" or "working group" to help facilitate and resource the growth and development of a youth ministry of some sort?

In considering necessary changes to a congregation's structure we should pay some attention to Gary McIntosh's observation that, "Whatever structure is selected it should do two things: maximize ministry and minimize maintenance."[43] While maintenance is important it cannot replace the kinds of things that attract and keep visitors and newcomers. Ministries can be created that are inviting and educational in a way that attracts people. Educational and social opportunities can be provided that expose newcomers to the congregation in positive a way so that they feel welcome and willing to participate.

There may be some question about whether or not a congregation needs to hire a consultant to help them through this process to close or find renewal. Consultants can come in many different shapes and sizes. There may be a regional staff person affiliated with a denomination who can assist in this work. There may be someone who can be hired to facilitate the planning process and assist in implementation work that is necessary. The financial situation may affect whether or not a consultant can be hired.

One congregational leader has written "I was blessed and greatly advantaged ... to have a congregational consultant to help navigate what was for all of us uncharted territory."[44] The consultant can help navigate and can also be a listener. This listening role can be helpful in nurturing the conversation and storytelling that will be helpful if the decision is made to close the church. This receives more attention in the Chapter Five on Pastoral Care.

If the issue on the table is closure, the need for consulting assistance may be an area where the closure team assigned by the wider church can be a helpful presence for the congregation. A member of this closure team will hopefully have some facilitation skills that will be helpful in developing plans with the congregation. The closure teams can also he a helpful presence when decisions are needed or the congregation is having difficulty moving forward.

If a consultant is hired then several things need to be kept in mind. The job description must be focused on whatever needs to be done to develop the assessment; discernment and transition plan and facilitate the conversation. There is a need to identify what will be asked of this person and to ensure that the job is getting done. As we have mentioned in other areas, measuring the progress of the consultant will be difficult if the job description is vague and undefined.

When considering a consultant it may be helpful to ask neighboring congregations if they are interested in sharing in the work of creating a transition plan. For example, there were four congregations from one denomination on Calgary's North Hill; all within a short distance of one another, all felt a need to begin a conversation around their respective futures. This conversation eventually led to the hiring of a consultant and continuing discussion about what the future looked like for these four congregations. One of the possibilities for each of these congregations was the sharing of resources, or "clustering".

The thought was that an agreement would be negotiated where the four congregations would share staff and programming. Worship services would be combined and rescheduled to provide variety and specialization where people felt it was needed. One congregation could offer a course, for example, that would be open to more people and reduce the duplication of previous efforts. This sharing of resources could progress to a point where congregations could begin discussing the possibility of merger.

When it comes to the possibility of merging Terry

Foland writes, "merger should clearly be the result of members discerning what God is calling them to be and do and an effort to carry out an exciting new vision for the church."[45] In many ways, the consideration of a merger by two congregations is like a dating relationship. Over a certain period of time a level of knowledge and intimacy develops that helps the two individuals make some important decisions about their futures together. What are the gifts and assets that each congregation can offer? Each congregation examines and evaluates its respective visions and motivations and decides whether or not they are compatible with the other congregation(s). I don't want to stretch this too far but it can be a helpful image to keep in mind.

Merger not only means closure but also the creation of a new entity. The potential rewards can be tremendous, however merger has some significant challenges.

We have talked about the challenges a congregation can face in a changing world. We have discussed the developing health of a congregation as it faces these challenges. The health of a congregation can affect its ultimate viability. This Chapter has talked about the need to discern the viability of a congregation and consider the possibility of developing a plan to help either confirm or refute this diagnosis. Information gained from a transition plan can assist in making the decision whether or not to close the congregation. We examine this decision making process in the next chapter.

Checklist

- Congregations reach crisis points in which important questions must be asked concerning viability.
- One of the goals of these questions can be the identification of the nature of the problem. There are several ways in which this "problem" can be identified.

- Review Annual Reports and other documents to find any trends affecting the viability of the congregation.
- Consult denominational officials for possible assistance in analyzing the trends that are identified.
- Ask whether or not the resources are present to create a transition plan that will test whether or not the congregation can thrive and grow. Is there a piece of property that can be sold to finance the plan? Are there any funds that can be accessed to provide the necessary support?
- Create the transition plan or move directly to the decision phase as discussed in Chapter Two.

Endnotes

1. McIntosh, Gary L. "Biblical Church Growth" (Grand Rapids, 2003), p. 152
2. Ibid., p. 155
3. Ibid. p.156
4. Ibid. p. 158
5. "Many Parishes Seem Closure Candidates" Boston Globe December 10th, 2003
6. Ibid.
7. For a more detailed inventory check out Appendix B in "Discerning Your Congregation's Future".
8. Interim Report of the Study Group to Research Denominational Membership Decline, 2000-126th General Assembly of the Presbyterian Church In Canada, p.2
9. "Many Parishes Seem Closure Candidates" Boston Globe December 10th, 2003
10. "Ending With Hope", Ed. Betty Anne Gaede (Bethesda, 2002), p.18

11. Barker, Ralph "The Royal Flying Corps in World War One" (London, 2002 Ed.), P.225

12. "Death and Birth In The Parish", Ed. Martin Marty et al (St. Louis, 1964), p.99

13. Kuhl, David "What Dying People Want" (Toronto, 2002), P.209

14. McIntosh, P. 15

15. "Ending With Hope, p. 18

16. Malphurs, Aubrey "Planting Growing Churches for the Twenty-First Century" (Grand Rapids, 1998), P.29

17. Marty, p.35

18. As suggested in a resource entitled "Is It Time to Fold the Tent?" p.3

19. Leas, Speed B. "Leadership and Conflict" (Nashville, 1982), P.84

20. Haugk, Kenneth C. "Antagonists in the Church" (Minneapolis, 1988), P.101

21. Ibid. p.102

22. Drucker, Peter "Innovation and Entrepreneurship" (New York, 1985), p.149

23. Heschel, Abraham "Moral Grandeur and Spiritual Audacity" Ed. Susan Heschel (New York, 1996), P.20

24. Murray-Parkes, Colin "Bereavement: Studies of Grief In Adult Life" (London, 1998), P.209

25. Bridges, William "Transitions" (Reading, 1980), P.4

26. Ibid. p. 11

27. Harland, Gordon "Engaging the Issues Before Us With Confidence and Hope" Touchstone, January 2003

28. Ibid.

29. Dudley, Carl "Where Have All the People Gone?" (New York, 1979), p.67

30. Marty, p.37

31. New Brunswick Reader June 15th, 2002

32. Ian Black Website: "Calling Time, Notes On Closing A Church"

33. Ibid.

34. "Whither the Downtown Montreal Churches" Anglican Journal, May, 2003

35. Ibid.

36. Schaller, Lyle "Tattered Trust: Is There Hope For Your Denomination?" (Nashville, 1996), P.26

37. Anderson, Terry "End Of Life Decisions" in Touchstone, January 2003

38. Swanson, Eric "Great To Good Churches" in Leadership, Spring 2003

39. Ibid.

40. Ibid.

41. Drucker, p. 228

42. Anderson, p.26

43. McIntosh, P.155

44. "Ending With Hope", p. 44

45. Ibid. p.64

Chapter Two
Decision

Daniel Goleman tells the story of a Catholic school facing serious financial problems. These challenges were reaching a crisis point in which the local archbishop saw few alternatives. Having considered all of the possibilities he made the difficult decision to close the school and assigned the head of the Catholic schools in that district to carry through with this difficult task. This director could have closed the school immediately. Students could have arrived the next day and find the doors locked and signs telling them what to do next.

The director chose another way, however. She called a meeting of teachers and staff and informed them of the problems and choices. They talked about the possibility of keeping the school open and what it would take to thrive. She listened as they offered their thoughts and opinions on the matter. This process was repeated with members of both the affected families and the wider community. When the round of meetings was complete the decision to close the school was allowed to stand. The students were reassigned to other Catholic schools and the doors were closed for the last time.[1]

The school would have inevitably closed. The difference was in how this closure happened. The process chosen for making the decision was the key. Instead of simply closing the doors and transferring people to other locations another decision-making process was chosen. People intimately involved with this school were invited to meet and discuss the situation. They were asked for their thoughts and opinions that were both heard and considered. People were included in the decision that had to be made. This story reminds us of the importance of making good decisions. It also reminds us of the importance of developing a process that is open and inclusive of the people intimately involved with the situation in question. Important decisions are not always quick and easy. They take a lot of time and hard work to accomplish.

The previous chapter helped us test the thought that our congregation may be in a troubled state. There is a time when we need to weigh the evidence and think about what the information is telling us. People in the congregation must have the opportunity to review the results of any viability tests and transition plan so they can make important decisions around the future of their congregation.

Interpreting these numbers and the final decision itself may be in the hands of denominational officials such as the bishop mentioned earlier. The ideal, however, is when the congregation can make its own decision. This is an opportunity for the local congregation and the wider church to build a relationship in which effective communication and pastoral care are important priorities. A congregation needs support for what it is about to do. We need to have the confidence that we are not closing a congregation that still has the potential to rebound and do some healthy and life giving things. We need to have some confidence that we have done the best that we can. The circumstances may be clear enough that a transition plan is unnecessary. There may be a trend in the congregation's finances that points all too clearly to a problem for which there may be no solutions. There may be an attendance issue that helps tell a clear story. There may be realities beyond the congregation that force the issue in a way that is all too clear.

There was a local congregation that was well situated on a major street. It was visible and had excellent access from this major artery. A decision was made by city traffic planners, however, that promised to bring an end to this situation. In fact, the building itself was scheduled for demolition. The street was going to be widened and the church property was needed to make this road construction project possible. With property being so expensive in this inner city area there was little chance of finding an equivalent location anywhere near the present site. The only clear options seemed to be merging with a nearby congregation of the same denomination or moving away from the area completely. The decision was made to merge with the neighbouring congregation as a way of maintaining some ministry presence in the area.

Whether the situation is simple or complicated, communication becomes an important part of the relationship between the denomination and congregation. Rollo May talks about the importance of language and communication in changing times in his book "Power and Innocence". May writes, "When an age is in the throes of profound transition, the first thing to disintegrate is language."[2] When we try and build relationships between congregations and their respective denominations language becomes important. This is especially true for when crises are experienced and something has to be done in response. We need to put some thought into the kinds of words we are going to use when establishing and maintaining communication with individuals and congregations.

This communication can be established and maintained in many ways. Perhaps one of the most important ways of doing this is by holding meetings in which parishioners can discuss important issues and participate in decision-making. These meetings offer opportunities for information sharing and the exchange of ideas. They offer opportunities in which people can ask questions that will help them learn more about the situation. They can even be places where people can air their disagreements and sharing their feelings.

There seems to be a tendency in the church to shy away from debate and disagreement. I have heard people claim that their goal in any meeting is to achieve a sense of "harmony" among the gathered people. There are times when harmony is important. There are also times, however, when people have to place their cards on the table and consider the various sides of an issue. These discussions can concern something as simple as the colours to be used for an upcoming paint job. Patrick Lencioni has written a series of excellent books on leadership. In "The Five Temptations of a C.E.O." he discusses the importance of debate and conflict in meetings. He comments on the desire for harmony but also notes that this only prevents healthy discussion and the effective decision-making these exchanges can produce.[3]

It is important that the denomination be represented at any of these meetings. This is to support the people present and clarify any concerns and uncertainties they may have. The denominational representatives can try to respond to questions and share any relevant information they possess. If they cannot help with certain questions then they can participate in the ongoing search for answers. The representatives can also hear the different ideas and opinions being expressed by the group. The physical presence of denominational officials can reassure parishioners that they will not be making their way through this process alone.

These meetings can be held at the church and they can also be held in people's homes. There are times when some issues cannot be addressed in a forum in which a large number of people are gathered. Smaller groups can offer safety and opportunity for parishioners to ask their questions and discuss the situation without a lot of people watching them. Smaller groups can help build a sense that people can have a say in what is unfolding. Making both options available can offer people a chance to choose a venue that is best for them. These venues can include places like local coffee shops and people's living rooms. Home group meetings can include things that can't easily be done in a wider and larger group, such as prayer, Bible study, refreshments and discussion.

These meetings will increase the workload of a congregation and denominational officials but they are an important way to hear from as many affected people as possible. Meeting in small groups may also provide a comfortable setting that helps reduce the potential for conflict. Regardless, every meeting should be documented with names and decisions officially recorded. Notes can be made about action items and the people responsible for accomplishing these tasks. Meetings should also be properly called so that people have the opportunity to fit them into their schedules. It will also be important to notify as many people as possible so that more voices can be heard.

When people do not have a say in decisions around valued institutions such as a congregation long-term problems can develop. In "Power and Innocence" Rollo May discusses the relationship between power and aggression. When we feel powerless and apathetic, we can also experience aggression. May writes, "As we make people powerless, we promote their violence rather than its control." Keeping an individual or group "out of the loop", so to speak, can increase the chances of anger and conflict.[4]

It is important that people in the congregation listen to the different voices, thoughts and opinions around them. This listening can happen in the small groups as I have just suggested. This listening can also happen when people gather in larger groups. As we engage in the conversation and debate it is also important to hear from representatives of the wider church. These representatives can offer helpful insights and information that will assist the decision-makers in their task.

There should be some consideration as to whether or not follow-up meetings would be appropriate. These follow-up meetings would deal with emerging issues such as changing attendance and financial situations. They could help parishioners through disagreements that may come about as the congregation looks ahead to a vote and a decision. Again, these meetings should be properly documented.

A letter or progress report at this early stage of the process may help clarify any questions and misunderstandings. There will be groups of people unable to attend the various meetings yet still be interested in knowing what happens. These include people in hospital, on planned trips away from their community, or people with limited mobility. For those unable to attend meetings there can be a report produced so that people can access the information. This kind of report of what took place can be in the form of a letter as we have mentioned earlier and can include a summary of what was said and any actions to be taken as a result of the discussion. This document can also include recommendations for future gatherings of both the congregation and the denomination.

Who communicates this news? It is not unusual for an organization to have an appointed spokesperson to deal with public communication. Who will stand in front of the gathered congregation and share with them the news and any other information they may require? When the transition plan reaches a point where the decision has to be made and communicated, a person can be identified as the one to inform the congregation and the wider church. In most cases this could be a leader selected by a congregation's board or it could be the clergyperson serving the congregation in question.

This assumes that there continues to be a working relationship between the clergyperson and the board. Emotions and conflict may reach a point where this relationship breaks down and some other option has to be considered. We'll be talking more about this kind of situation later.

Communicating this decision may be a difficult and emotional moment for both the spokesperson sharing the information and the people who are receiving this news for the first time. There will be a real need for empathy and compassion. There will be a need to deal with the possibility of an angry response. David Kuhl has written, "Hearing bad news often results in anger—at change, at information, at life, illness, mortality, and, finally, the messenger."[5] He goes on to write, "Thus, one must ask, what is the best way of giving and receiving information that is difficult to hear?" So much depends on the kind of relationships within and beyond the congregation.

One of my favourite poets is John Donne. In one of his sonnets he writes, "No man is an island". This is true of individual people as they relate to family and community. This is also true of congregations as they relate to the wider denominations in which they participate. The main thing to remember is that the congregation is not alone as they make these important decisions around closure. Connections are important at a time like this. The wider church has an important place in this process, as there are often people and resources available to assist the closing congregation. This can include the work of both assessing viability and making the necessary decisions about this viability. Denominations may have policies and procedures that need to be considered in any decision making process. Knowledgeable and competent resource people will be able to help sort much of this out. Denominations can also ensure that decisions are made in a timely fashion. Meetings may need to be called and chaired and these are sometimes time consuming tasks that cannot be left until the last minute. There are times when the wider church has to assert itself and actually initiate the decision making process.

The United Brethren denomination states that, "The

process for closing a church can be initiated by: A) The local board of administration. The board will notify the conference superintendent of its desire, and the local board and superintendent will begin discussing the idea. B) The conference council may direct the superintendent to meet with a local board about the possibility of closing the church. C) The conference superintendent may call a local conference to discuss the possibility of closing the church."[6] In the Episcopal Church, the congregation itself initiates any efforts to close.[7]

One of the important things to impress upon the spokesperson communicating the decision to the congregation in question is that they have to make a commitment to be up front and honest about what is going on. We need to communicate our decision in a way in which the affected congregation will know and somehow understand that we are telling them the truth about what is going to be happening. In many ways it is no different than a doctor trying to share a diagnosis with a patient. When dealing with a dying patient Heather Robertson writes, "The dying patient's first task is to receive and understand the truth, and the doctor's obligation is to tell the truth as the patient wants to hear it."[8] People have the right to be informed and know what's going on. The same is true of people in a closing congregation. As we have previously mentioned, we have to be honest and ensure that the information we are sharing is accurate and clear. We also have to be careful in maintaining any confidences that develop as a result of the overall process.

When these conversations arise around whether or not a congregation needs to close, the kind of information that will be shared needs to be stated firmly and often. Clarity and persistence become important considerations here. Those who may be hearing this news for the first time may be shocked to a point of being unable to process the information. Doctors often experience the need to repeat a diagnosis because the patient became shocked to the point of finding the news unbelievable. There are things that we do not want to hear. There are realities that we find difficult to face. These kinds of defensive mechanisms can be factored in to the planning around what to do with information.

There were people who found the news of my previous congregation's closure difficult. There were a number of people who were not surprised. The various annual reports and board updates were painting a picture that was becoming increasingly clear. The building, itself, was showing visible signs of wear and tear. Attendance and the offering were largely unchanged in the face of increasing capital costs and inflation.

There were also people who refused to believe that my previous congregation would close. There were those who were constantly searching for ways of rescuing the congregation. Even after the decision to close was officially accepted by the denominational executive in our area, there were those who went door to door and set up information tables at a nearby grocery store to try and recruit new members. Desperation set in for some who refused to believe the news that the congregation would be closing. Jennie Wilting writes, "One way people unnecessarily create problems for themselves is by refusing to accept and deal with reality."[9] Reality, in this case, is the way the world actually is. The sun rises in the East and sets in the West whether we like it or not. It's reality and we need to work with it. We cannot change reality. When the tire on my car is flat I need to change it or there will be more serious problems later on down the road. Wilting adds, "It is worthwhile to take some time to try to determine what reality is in a particular situation."

I am not suggesting that everyone agree with the decision and simply move on with their lives. This would ignore the reality of loss and grief that is present in this situation. It would also ignore the reality that people may not agree with what is going on. I think we would be hard pressed to find any decision to close a church that was unanimous. These are realities that we will be examining later but they also need to be considered here. There will be many different responses to the news that the congregation is going to close and we need to be aware of these potential responses. Perhaps a group from the wider church can help deal with these possibilities.

In the previous chapter I briefly introduced the concept of a closure team. This is a group of people assigned by the denomination to which the closing congregation belongs. It's a group of people assigned to share the closure process with the congregation in question. Their level of involvement can be left to their discretion. William Hobgood writes, "…it serves a judicatory well to have either a special task force or a standing group charged with the task of gathering information so that members will hear wise and accurate answers to their myriad questions."[10] Hobgood adds, "In the Presbyterian Church (U.S.A.), for example, the congregation's presbytery will name an administrative commission which will work with the congregation in legal, ecclesiastical and spiritual matters related to the closing."

This idea of a closure team is based on this practice of the Presbyterian Church (USA). It is also based on practices from within disciplines such as palliative care. In palliative care a group of people representing different professions would assemble to help meet the medical needs of dying people. Heather Robertson talks about a hospice in the Ottawa area called "Hospice of All Saints".[11] This is a place with a Multi Disciplinary Team serving their patients. Robertson writes, "Each week the team monitors the status of the … patients on the hospice caseload." This idea of a Multi-Disciplinary Team goes back to the work of Dame Cicely Saunders at London's St. Christopher's Hospice. These teams are being created with increasing frequency because they have proven to be effective.[12] This is where we can take this idea of a Multi-Disciplinary Team and apply it to the closing of a congregation.

A denomination can even find their own name for the group if they like. There may be rules and guidelines about what this group can be called. There may be regulations affecting their membership and job description as well. A denomination will need to show some care when selecting the name of the team working with a closing congregation. One denomination needing to work with a closing congregation sent in a group called the "Trauma Team". This name conjures up ideas and images that are not always consistent with the work that they will be trying to accomplish. It was because of this kind of confusion that the gifts and skills of the "trauma team" were not used to their best advantage.

For the purposes of this book I was wondering what to name this group when a family member suggested I simply call it a "closure team". One of the reasons why I suggest and support the creation of a "closure team" is the result of my previous experience. People were assigned by the wider denomination in random fashion to assist with the closing of the congregation. However, there was no real coordination between these individuals and there was no leadership. There was nothing that held these individuals together as one cohesive group or team. It is now obvious that a group like this requires a balance of skills and experience in leadership, coaching, organizing and coordinating. This combination of skills and experience will help the group work as an effective team.

The closure team would have a number of major responsibilities. This team would provide support and be an advocate for the people in the closing congregation.[13] It would offer counsel when important questions need to be addressed as well as offer guidance, companionship and leadership.[14] When my previous congregation closed presbytery made a pastoral care worker available to be a helpful presence for when decisions were being made. People were experiencing the stress and difficulties of this process and the pastoral care person was someone to whom they could talk. In this particular case, the pastoral care worker was present at any important meetings taking place. She was also present at one of the healing services that we held in anticipation of the closure. The combined work of denominational staff and the closure team can be an important "sign of the unity and wholeness of the church."[15] It can be a visible sign that the church is a part of the wider body of Christ.

Another role that the closure team can assume is that of protector. This will be dealt with in more detail when we reach the chapter on "Conflict" but a couple of things can be mentioned here. Emotions can run pretty high in a closing congregation. Things can be said and done that are potentially harmful. Hobgood writes, "When a congregation is fragile enough to be near its end, it may need protection from those outside who want the property, or those inside who just want to avoid any responsibility for the congregation's failing life."[16] There will be times when protection is necessary from congregations and individuals wanting the assets for their own purposes. Requests for assets may be appropriate but these should be processed through the proper channels. Denominational officials can wait until the proper time and then present the possible options for the assignment of any assets made available through the sale of property, etc.

The denomination can provide educational opportunities for people in the congregation and the team named to work with them. People can learn more about things like grief and conflict. They can learn more about the beliefs and ways of doing things within their denomination. We can get so caught up in the life and work of the congregation we lose touch with the wider church. We may be unaware of simple things like how the denomination is managed, and so on. It is important that the members and leaders of a congregation become familiar with any manuals and handbooks made available by the denomination. This helps with the coordination between the congregation and the wider church.

When people have a chance to learn more about these important topics then it reduces the possibility of conflict and later difficulties. We'll talk more about this in later chapters but it can be said here that people named by the wider church have to be "well informed"[17] about what is going on and what they are getting in to. A part of this education task may be the gathering, managing and sharing of information about church closures. The closure team could plan and carry out a retreat with the main goal being education and relationship building. A guide could help them prepare for the task and challenges ahead.

One of the challenges will be people's need for news and information. Parishioners will want to know what is going on and how this developing situation will affect them. A colleague involved in a number of church closures has told me that one of the challenges facing the closure team will be the number of phone calls and e-mails that will be received. Some people will be requesting information while others will be simply airing grievances. Will this mean that one person will be designated as the one whom people can call when they have questions and concerns? While this kind of communication is important it can also be time consuming for those with commitments in other places. Resources must be managed wisely so that burnout of volunteers doesn't deprive the process of people who can help things along.

If members of the team are to be effective then one of the things that they have to deal with are their own feelings. This is an extremely emotional time and we need to be prepared for this consideration of both the congregation's and our own thoughts and feelings about many things. It may not be so much a question of confronting our mortality as dealing with another's sadness and anger. How are we going to respond when people start shouting at us? How do we respond to insults and name-calling? These are important matters to consider.[18]

As we continue with our discussion about workload and challenges we can also deal with the numbers and composition of the closure team. I would suggest the team be made up of no more than between five and seven people. There has to be enough to cover any holidays or sabbaticals that come along. There also needs to be a number of people available in case certain responsibilities need to be assumed by the team. Some congregations will need a group of people replacing the board or trustees. There may be a level of conflict that requires a high level of participation from the team. There may be situations, however, when five members may be too many. In congregations where there is a significant level of agreement with the decisions being made there may be an opportunity to reduce this number to three. So much depends on the individual situation. Decisions around the size of the closure teams can be made when they are being appointed. They can also be changed, as the situation requires. These decisions can also be made in consultation with the congregation in question. It is important to maintain a high level of flexibility as the situation can change rapidly.

This constantly changing landscape is why the closure team needs to consist of a group of people with a fairly wide-ranging collection of gifts and skills. This is consistent with Paul's observation in First Corinthians in which he discusses the different gifts that people have with which to share with their faith community.[19] Some people will be effective in situations where there is conflict. Others may see their gifts as being helpful in other ways. Variety is important when choosing the closure team.

I suggest the above number of members for the closure team because too many people may be counterproductive. Wilting writes, "Problems can be created and the size of the problem increased by involving too many people."[20] Wilting goes on to suggest, "At times, to involve other people in a particular problem, you increase (the problem's) size." There seems to be a fine line between having too many people and just enough.

When it comes to the closure team that we have been discussing there has been an identified need for the members sharing a balance of experience and skill. This combination of skill and experience can be in areas such as administration, conflict management, facilitation, leading worship and listening. It is also important to note that this team has to be ready for anything, including the threat of violence. Emotions may boil to a point where extreme feelings are expressed in inappropriate ways. Lines may be crossed and people hurt because of this. Safety has to be a constant consideration. One can hope that this kind of extreme response will never happen. Unfortunately, we must still plan for this possibility.

The situation may reach a point in which the wider church has to step in and take charge. When this step is taken the tension in the congregation may rise to a point where people may become fearful of what is happening around them. There may be some ugly scenes where concerns are justified and the job of responding will fall to people beyond the congregation. With no coherent plan these people may not know how to respond to a growing crisis. The closure team assigned to the congregation would have the information and training necessary to become a front line player when these situations escalate. They have worked at establishing a relationship with the congregation and could assume key leadership roles in helping restore troubling situations. Some sort of crisis management training may need to be arranged for at least one of the closure team members. The denomination, in general, should have plans for any crisis they may face. The wider church can be consulted while developing these plans as they have the experience and people who can offer constructive input.

When the closure team encounters a situation, there may have to be a decision around whether or not this is something that they will need to deal with immediately. Is a given situation something that the team needs to address or is this something that can be handled within the congregation? There are some problems that cannot wait for a meeting to be called and agenda established. The closure team will have to be proactive. We will have a closer look at some of these issues in the chapter on "Conflict". It is also appropriate to deal with it here, as there may be some crisis points reached during meetings and while the decisions are being made.

As we continue with our discussion of closure teams we can consider the relationship they have with their respective denominations. The closure team can produce and submit a series of progress reports to the wider church concerning the congregation to which it has been assigned. These reports can be followed up with a final report outlining experiences and learnings gained by the closure team in its work with the congregation. The closure team can also help their denomination build a strategy for working with any future closures. This is important as so many denominations work with groups that don't always have a good institutional memory. People come and go. Not everyone has the time and energy necessary to see this kind of process through. The closure team can build a series of policies and procedures that can assist in any future efforts. They can also ensure that any policies and procedures remain as current as possible. This can be important as the denomination may find itself in the place where it needs to do things like listing and selling property. Decisions will need to be made about what can be dealt with by the closure team and what will need to be addressed at higher levels of the denomination. Denominational standards may be clear on these issues, and yet, there may be times in which some interpretation required. Interpretation can be done by either the closure team itself or denominational officials with skill and experience in a given area of expertise.

As we consider the possible challenges, we can see how the concept of grace can play an important part of this difficult decision making process. Grace is that reality in which goodwill is shown between people. Grace requires a lot of effort as we deal with a situation that tries our patience to a breaking point. One thing we can remember is that we are all on the same team and have the congregation's best interests at heart. Working together in difficult times requires a tremendous amount of compassion, forgiveness and understanding. Celia Sandys and Jonathan Littman talk about this in their book on Winston Churchill and the leadership he offered. They discussed his ability to build relationships and work his way through conflict so that a higher goal could be met.[21] With thoughts such as these supporting our work we can relate with people in a way that helps reduce tension and conflict.

We may not hear enough about grace in the church. This is especially true when we look ahead to a significant congregational decision such as whether or not to close. We need to be patient with one another's mistakes. We need to be open to differing ideas and opinions. We need to be forgiving. We can see these as being "givens" as we profess to be a Christian people. These "givens" can go out the window, however, when the tension increases. We need to show some patience and self-control when we face the temptation to yell and scream.

When considering the decision to close it is also important that we remember to pray. We may forget about the One who is a sure and constant presence throughout this difficult and challenging time. Abraham Heschel has written, "Some of our deepest insights, decisions and attitudes are born in moments of prayer."[22] Prayer can help us remain centered and focused on the issues at hand. A time of prayer can also help us stay in touch with God and God's hopes and dreams for all of us. On those occasions, for example, when we find it difficult to know whether or not we are worshipping God or the building prayer can help us keep our bearings. We can be reminded of our commitments and our priorities. We can be reminded of the important relationships that help support us.

There are some other important questions to be considered as we make the necessary decisions around closure. One of these questions concerns the people making the decision. Individual congregations and denominations will have guidelines around who can vote in certain situations. If your congregation does not have any of these guidelines in place then the denomination can provide some options. At my previous congregation it came down to a members only vote. Membership is something that may vary from one denomination to another. Membership may or may not be a requirement for these kinds of decisions in some denominations. It is important to find out so people will know where they stand.

We have to be careful about the legal requirements identified by both our denomination and the government jurisdiction in which our congregation exists. When my previous congregation had its congregational meeting we were surprised to find out that a number of our more active people were not actually members and this affected their ability to vote. This also had an effect on how they responded to the decision. It is important to remind people of the need to confirm whether or not they are members of a congregation. A person may be under the impression that they are members simply because they actively contribute to the life of the congregation. Others may be under the impression that contributing financially is an automatic inclusion in the membership roles.

It isn't a question of wanting to exclude people from this critical decision. There are often legalities both within and outside a denomination that need to be considered as well. Inviting people to confirm their membership status will reduce the possibility of last minute confusion and also provide the opportunity to educate people as to the denominational requirements for membership. A simple review of any available membership lists may be a helpful way of preparing for a vote.

One caution I would note is that there may be a temptation to push through a quick membership class so that people will be able to have a say in the decision-making. While this may be appropriate for people who have been active over a certain period of time it may only cause further problems for people recently coming in to a congregation. As word of a possible closure circulates through a community, some newcomers may arrive with the misguided but well-meaning mission of somehow reversing any kind of closure decision. These kinds of last minute efforts will be discussed in a later chapter but it is an important consideration here, as there may be some implications for any vote that has to be taken.

Another question that can be dealt with here is the one around the people and parties benefiting from a particular closure. When the wider denomination voted to accept my previous congregation's decision to close, suspicions were raised that this was a money grab to help finance new ministries in other areas of the city. This would be no different than the local school boards closing schools in one area to free up capital dollars to build in other places that need attention. This comparison was made during a press conference where representatives of the wider church used this as one of the reasons why this particular congregation was closing.

This concern about outside interests may introduce a conversation around justice issues. Should a congregation close to release assets, people and energy for new efforts somewhere else? Is this simply a case of a denomination sacrificing a viable congregation for resources to be used in another way? This is where the sharing of clear and honest information also becomes important. It's all too easy to circulate misinformation that feeds people's preconceived notions. Once this information gets out it is almost impossible to put the genie back in the bottle. Spreading rumors can be one of the ways people work at resisting the decision to close their congregation.

It is hard to predict the intensity of the response from people. Some people may be surprised that their congregation is closing, and some may even be relieved. It is almost impossible to predict how people will react when the question is raised for discussion and possible decision-making. They may have known that there were serious problems that needed to be addressed. There may have been clues that have been included in previous annual reports or board minutes. There may have been conversations in which people have pointed to a changing community or financial situation. Many people may have been waiting for these kinds of issues to be brought into the open so that they can figure out what is going on and respond in an appropriate way. We will deal with some of these responses in our chapter on grief.

Once a diagnosis is made, the doctor faces the task of assessing the condition of the patient. What is happening and how can the patient respond? Is there any way of treating the problem? In situations where the diagnosis is terminal some discussion can happen around the amount of time a person has left. There can also be some consideration of what the person needs to do in order to complete any unfinished business. There is a similar dynamic at work in a congregation that is facing the decision of whether or not to close.

Once a decision is made to close there can be an assessment of the financial picture and the energy available for the work outlined by the congregation. This assessment can help established a scheduled time for closure. It can give parishioners a sense of the time left to take care of necessary business. People may have questions about when the closure will likely happen and the amount of time available for getting the congregation's affairs in order.

Before we bring this part of our discussion to a close, another consideration that can be included here is the question of consulting legal counsel. A denomination may have to consult a lawyer as early in the process as possible. There may be certain legalities that need to be observed. There may be property issues needing to be addressed. I remember hearing of a congregation that was about to sell the house they had once provided for the minister. When they found the deed they suddenly discovered that the house was in the name of a former minister and not the congregation itself. It was a simple mistake and easy enough to remedy but it does remind us of the importance of making sure our legal paperwork is in order.

A lawyer can help deal with this kind of documentation and any regulations that a government may have for a situation in which a congregation closes. Non-profit organizations may come under different sets of rules and laws depending on where the congregation is located. These government rules and regulations may affect what can be done with the different assets a congregation may have.[23] The higher church could recommend the lawyer. There may be someone on the denominational staff who could be of assistance. Many denominations have legal professionals available when congregations require advice. Whoever is selected will have to acquaint themselves with the rules and requirements that will be followed as a result of a congregation's decision. It may be necessary to provide the lawyer with any relevant manuals or rulebooks so that his/her advice and information can be as grounded and practical as possible.

Any decision made by a congregation will set off an important round of planning. If the congregation votes to remain open then key viability issues have to be faced and overcome. There are implications in both the decisions to remain open and to close. I have told a number of groups through the years that the status quo is never an option in a situation of this nature. If the congregation votes to remain open then some effort will have to be made in planning what will happen towards keeping the doors open. There must be changes made to bring about change and growth. When a congregation votes to close then a round of planning will be necessary in making this an orderly process and help reduce the potential for conflict and unnecessary pain.

Planning a church closure will be the task to which we now turn our attention.

Chapter Two Checklist

- When the questions around the viability of a congregation have been dealt with the decision whether to close or remain open has to be made.
- This is a decision requiring the participation of all the stakeholders. Who are the stakeholders? How do they relate to the congregation in question?
- Meetings can be held in which these stakeholders consider the available information and options. Will these meetings be held in small groups? Will these meetings be held in people's homes or in a larger gathering place?
- A vote can then be held in which the decision is made in an official way. Who votes and how will this process be managed? How will the respective denomination participate in this voting process?
- How will this decision be processed by the denomination? What kind of official action is needed from the various levels of denominational management?
- This decision will affect the congregation in a way that will bring about change even it there is a vote to remain open.

Endnotes

1.   Goleman, Daniel et al "Primal Leadership" (Boston, 2002), p.66
2.   May, Rollo "Power and Innocence: A Search for the Sources of Violence" (New York, 1972), p.65
3.   Lencioni, Patrick "The Five Temptations of A C.E.O." (New York, 1998), pp. 59-73

4. May, p.23
5. Kuhl, David "What Dying People Want" (Toronto, 2002), p.58
6. United Brethren Discipline, 2001-2005
7. May 20, 2003 personal e-mail
8. Robertson, Heather "Meeting Death: In Hospital, Hospice and at Home" (Toronto, 2000), P.91
9. Wilting, Jennie "Nurse, Colleagues, and Patients: Achieving Congenial Interpersonal Relationships" (Edmonton, 1990), P. 15
10. "Ending With Hope", Betty Anne Goede Ed. (Bethesda, 2002), P.87
11. Robertson, P.182
12. Ibid, P.275
13. Auger, Jeanette A. "Social Perspectives On Death and Dying" (Halifax, 2000), P.97
14. Ending With Hope, P.25
15. Ibid., P. 79
16. Ibid., P.80
17. Ibid., P.79
18. Kuhl, P.56
19. 1 Corinthians 12: 4-11
20. Wilting, P. 17
21. Sandys, Celia and Littman, Jonathan "We Shall Not Fail: The Inspiring Leadership of Winston Churchill" (New York, 2003), P. 67-78
22. Heschel, Abraham "Moral Grandeur and Spiritual Audacity" (New York, 1996, p. 109
23. "Is It Time to Fold the Tent?", P. 3

Chapter Three
Planning

When I was assigned to my first congregation as an ordained minister I had to travel across Canada in order to reach the communities I would be serving. When preparing for this kind of journey, it is always a good idea to have a look at the road ahead to see what kind of trip this might be. One of the first things I did when told my destination was purchase some maps and go to a nearby coffee shop. I spread one of these maps out on a table and began the process of identifying the major highways I would be taking. I was looking for some of the places where I could visit and perhaps find a motel. I had some decisions to make. In looking at some of the maps I chose to pass through the major cities as quickly as possible. Using a hi-lighter, I found the shortest routes possible through some of the biggest metropolitan areas in Canada. I had never driven through any of these cities before so this was going to be quite an adventure.

The route that I had plotted worked out well for the first part of the journey. This continued to be the case until I reached the Montreal suburbs. My planned route looked straightforward enough. It was clearly marked and all I had to do was follow the bright yellow line. The only problem was that I had never been down any of these roads before and had no idea what they were like. As we all know, there is huge difference between what appears on a map and what really exists. I was thinking about this as I reached the banks of a river at a town just outside Montreal. The place was called Oka, and as I drove through this community I discovered that the only way across the river was a small, slow moving ferry. While I waited I realized that my hopes for a quick trip through the area were not going to work out the way that I had planned.

Good planning is an important part of anything we do. This includes both trips across the country and the simple things we do every day. This chapter will deal with planning and what can happen to help make the closure process as smooth as possible. This planning will help map the future once the decision to close has been made. Planning is something that is critical for the congregation facing closure. Planning is also critical for the wider denomination as well. People are able to identify the different tasks they have to accomplish. They can also bring a sense of order to the often-chaotic journey.

One of the first things to be done when the closure decision is made is to identify the people who will be involved in this planning process. This is important for both the congregation and the denomination. Who deals with important decisions around property and membership? Who ensures that staff is treated fairly? Who is accountable for what is going to be happening? This has to be a comprehensive piece of work because with this kind of effort any surprise can potentially derail the entire process and cause a lot of unnecessary pain and suffering.

Planning may seem like a boring and unnecessary task but considering the potential challenges, it is crucial. Planning the closure of a congregation can cover a lot of ground. A colleague once told me that we could never be too prepared for anything in life. I remember the last words of the ancient Greek philosopher Socrates, who is quoted as saying, "Criton, we owe a cock to Asclepios; pay it without fail".[1] This may seem like an unusual thing for someone like Socrates to say but in considering his terminal condition he had the presence of mind to take care of last minute details so that there would be fewer "loose ends" for those left behind. He did not want to leave anything to chance. Detailed plans are important. They not only take care of the routine matters in need of our attention, they help reduce the possibilities of long-term conflict. These possibilities present themselves in many different and perhaps surprising ways.

One afternoon I was having coffee with a parishioner. As we were bringing the conversation to a close she told me that she had one more thing that she needed to speak with me about. She mentioned the community newsletter that went out to homes in the area around the church location. She asked if I would submit an article to this newsletter talking about the congregation's decision to close the church and something about how this would affect the community. There had been a number of rumors going around about the situation so I agreed that it would be something that might be helpful. An article would be one way of offering news and information that helps people understand what has been happening. Follow-up articles could give the public an ongoing sense of what is happening. These can be discussed among the stakeholders when ongoing planning meetings are held.

I was able to make a submission to the community newsletter a couple of days later. It was an article dealing with the decision to close the congregation. It was brief and to the point. I had the chair of the board and a local denominational staff person have a look at it just to be sure. I didn't want to contribute anything that would only feed the already active rumour mill and wind up being counterproductive. With the approval of both individuals I sent the article off to the editor of the newsletter to be published in the Christmas edition. People had a chance to read what was happening before we reached the time of the Christmas Eve service.

I thought that the media involvement would end there. I was pretty naïve when it came to these things and was surprised by what happened next. A local radio news reporter read the newsletter article and felt that it would make an interesting "local interest" news story for her station. The reporter and I met at the church and taped an interview. She was able to include some comments from parishioners and staff. Some music from the church choir was also recorded. When the story ran on the radio a television station picked it up. They brought camera crews to the church and shot some footage and interviews. A couple of taped stories were aired on the evening television news.

All of this media exposure was something that we had not anticipated. It simply hadn't crossed our minds that this kind of thing could happen. It had not occurred to any of us that the closure of a congregation would have gained this much interest. We had not discussed the need to name a spokesperson. When it came time to deal with the media I found myself in that role by default. I had little idea of what I was going to say. I stammered through a couple of interviews and hoped for the best. This would cause trouble for me later on but it seemed like the thing to do at the time. It was important to tell our story to as many people in the community as possible to let them know what was truly going on and dispel any rumours. Unnecessary gossip and negative exposure would not help the situation or make things any easier for parishioners. This is why it is important that we consider some of these issues around dealing with the media.

It is important, as previously discussed, that someone be named to speak with the media and that this person be fully informed about what is going on with the closure. It is also important that this person be able to communicate in a way that is clear and organize their thoughts in a manner that reduces the potential for confusion and misunderstanding. They also need the ability to manage what they share, as there may be information that is confidential and therefore not appropriate for releasing to the public. They have to think on their feet. They will need some awareness of which questions are appropriate and which are inappropriate. Closing a congregation can be a very personal and painful effort for people and they may not want to be interviewed. A spokesperson can reduce, if not totally eliminate, the pressure for people to speak with a reporter. People have a choice as to whether or not they wish to be interviewed. When people in the media were approaching me for an interview there were times when I declined the offer. Some respected these wishes while other reporters became aggressive. Each of us has the right to say "no", and it is important to keep this in mind.

When dealing with the media, there may come a time when it is important to issue a press release of some kind. It may also be a helpful step to call a press conference. The kind of information that is released is important to the communication process. It continues the effort to reduce the amount of gossip and misinformation being circulated. It is also an important way of sharing another side of the story. When the wider church intervened during the closure of one of my previous congregations it became obvious that some sort of effort had to be made to counter some of the negative press that we were receiving. Stories fed to the media do not always pass through official channels. People in the congregation who were convinced that the church could be rescued were feeding biased stories to a local network, which in turn generated additional conflict. When this kind of conflict arises and it reaches the public's attention there can be a race between parties to control the information.

Two ways that are helpful in telling the story of what is happening are newspaper announcements and postings on official congregational websites. We have talked about some different types of media contact already. What we can discuss here are simple announcements that do not require detailed explanation or clarification. Information concerning things like worship service times can be shared through both of these mediums for members and the general public.

Each congregation can develop a way of communicating with the people around them. We have mentioned the possibilities of community newsletter and congregational websites in addition to news media. Another possibility is the creation of a phone tree. A phone tree is a process by which parishioners on the congregation's contact list are phoned on a regular basis by callers recruited from within the same congregation. It's relatively simple to create. The first step is easy. All we have to do is add up the number of names on the contact list. The second step is to find out how many people are interested and available to make a number of phone calls to people in the congregation. When we know the number of available callers then this list can be divided accordingly. A congregation with 50 people on their contact list, for example, may be able to recruit 5 callers. This means that each caller will have up to ten phone calls to make.

I will make one cautionary note here. Some people on the contact list may not want this kind of attention. So it may be wise to obtain permission before placing a name and phone number on a caller's contact list. It may be prudent to check into any laws in place regarding privacy before handing over names and phone numbers to callers.

Training for these callers can be arranged with the help of denominational staff. This training can help make the phone calls an important contribution to the life of the congregation. These calls can find out how people are responding to the situation. These calls can also ensure that information is making its way through to the people who need it the most.

Planning the closure of a congregation includes both individuals and the committees they serve. There may be individuals and groups within each congregation with particular responsibilities in these kinds of situations. There may be a finance committee, for example, with the responsibility of closing the books when the appropriate time arrives. They will also be responsible for arranging things like final audits. The finance committee may be one group that will have to schedule a meeting with the closure team in order to review the particular tasks it will have to accomplish within a given time frame.

When my previous congregation made the decision to close there was some uncertainty about what each group and committee needed to do. How were the trustees to relate to the congregation and presbytery when it came to listing and selling the building and dispersing the congregation's assets? When the congregation and the wider church agree on a process by which the closing will be managed, a written agreement should be developed. This agreement would help reduce the risk of any misunderstandings or conflicts that may occur as the process moves along. The closure team would have a central role in ensuring the completion of this agreement.

One example of how this closure team can help the congregation fulfill its agreements and commitments is by supporting and advocating for the closing congregation and its people. Jeanette Auger explains that this is something that happens when a team of people cares for a dying human being.[2] Please note that I am not offering a direct comparison between a dying human being and a closing congregation. There are similarities we can consider, however. There may be a time, for example, when the closure team needs to assume the daily management of the congregation. The legal term that describes this work is "proxy". A proxy is a person with the legal authority to make decisions on behalf of another person. Like the situation involving an individual person, there may be a time when the congregation can no longer manage its day-to-day affairs so the proxy, or closure team, would step in. The closure team and congregation can negotiate the terms of what this kind of intervention would involve and when it would be appropriate. It would be advisable to document these terms. This document would constitute a kind of "Living Will". Living wills are increasingly popular and help identify a person's wishes when they are no longer capable of expressing them.

One of the early contributions that the closure team can make is in helping the congregation choose the time when they will need to have their affairs completed and in order. Timing is important. A congregation will have commitments and responsibilities that require an adequate amount of time to deal with appropriately. People will also be considering their futures in terms of the new congregations they will be attending. They will need time to look for new places to worship and to adjust to the changes they will be facing. They may find losing their church difficult. While age may not determine the level of difficulty in dealing with change, older people may find this particular experience difficult. Lawrence Whalley suggests that older people, especially, "are less efficient in their responses to rapid environmental change".[3] While this may be the case from a scientific and anecdotal point of view, we cannot allow ourselves to buy into generalized thinking about certain age groups. I have seen people of all ages resist change of any kind. People of all ages will need time to adjust.

There will have to be enough time set aside for planning, providing pastoral care and making arrangements for any closing services and activities that folks in the congregation name as being important for them. There are other realities such as the listing and selling of properties in the congregation's possession. While some of this could be done after the official closing it is important to give parishioners as much input as possible.

Another reason why timing is important is that a prolonged closure is not always helpful. We cannot allow closing congregations to languish. In palliative care circles it is not appropriate to unnecessarily prolong the dying of an individual.[4] This is important to keep in mind for churches as well. When the closing process is prolonged there is an increasing chance of unnecessary pain and conflict. An extensive consultation between denomination and congregation may be necessary to finding the most helpful closing date. These discussions can be documented so they can be a helpful reference as the closing process develops.

When sharing in the work of closing a congregation the closure team members should be keeping notes for evaluation and future use. It is important that we maintain records of what has happened and to note any observations and learnings that may help in future efforts to assist closing congregations. Past records could offer information and reassurance that could help assist in the work of the congregation, closure team and wider denomination. Heather Robertson mentions the binder that Victoria Hospice has issued.[5] This binder contains important information about a person's options. It also lists available services and contact numbers.

The process of dealing with this amount of planning, feedback and information will require a number of meetings between the people in the congregation and the closure team. The members of the congregation can determine the frequency of these meetings, as they will be the ones in a position to help control the process. The closure team will also have issues requiring attention. These meetings can be called to consider future plans and options. Depending on how things are progressing, these meetings can typically take place on a regular basis. They can help establish a relationship between the congregation and the closure team. They can also build communication and trust. This is where it is important that at least one member of the closure team be skilled at facilitating meetings. It's the facilitator's job to ensure that conversation flows and that everyone has his or her say.

The planning process will be developed within the meetings between the congregation and closure team. Flexibility is an important consideration when establishing an agenda. There will be a lot of material to cover and a number of voices to hear. These meetings can establish action plans and name the people responsible for certain tasks. They can set timelines, goals and tasks so that the process can unfold in an orderly fashion.

One of the most important things that can happen at these meetings is that communication be established and maintained between the congregation and the wider denomination. Each meeting can begin with a "check-in" time where the team is brought up to date on what is happening in the congregation. The team can assess the progress of the planning and closure process. Problems can be identified and dealt with accordingly. Emerging issues can be dealt with in a prompt, effective manner. The team can also help with any change in plans.

In building this relationship between closure team and parishioners, the congregation can also offer some background as to the congregation's history, and some of the events leading up to the decision to close. Financial papers can be reviewed as well as minutes from recent board meetings. There may be other kinds of documentation that will be important for the closing process. This gives people a chance to put their cards on the table and increase the level of openness between the different groups. It is a time for telling stories and building relationships. It is a time for sharing important information. All of these things can help contribute to the overall agenda. This sharing can also reduce the number of surprises that can sometimes be experienced.

As previously mentioned the plans developed at these meetings can take into consideration the people who will be affected by this closure. Who ministers to the members and where will they go? We have discussed possibilities such as the creation of a phone tree. Part of our effort can help parishioners look ahead to the future. When considering a new congregation for people it may be helpful to ask some important questions. Perhaps the first question concerns belief. What do we believe about God? What do we believe about Jesus and doctrine such as the resurrection? These questions are important because not all congregations are the same when it comes to what they believe. Not all clergy preach the same thing. Some congregations tend to be more liberal or conservative then others. A person may feel more at home in one type of church as opposed to another. It is helpful to ask around. Parishioners can be invited to visit churches their friends and family attend. They can be encouraged to visit area congregations within the same denomination. They can also be encouraged to speak with the clergy in these congregations. It may be possible to set up an appointment to speak with one of the staff in a new congregation so that some important questions can be answered. One of the realities of our present age is that people "shop" for churches. They go from congregation to congregation in search of the place where they will feel at home. People want to be accepted and cared for and this is why many will drive long distances for worship and a community in which they can find a place.

There are many different reasons around why people attend or join a particular church. They may be attending as a result of a friend's invitation. They may have attended an important wedding or funeral there. It may be something as simple as the convenient location or the amenities such as a wheelchair ramp or elevator. When moving to another congregation one can ask some questions about what is being offered. One congregation may have a reputation as having a strong addictions recovery program while another may specialize in ministering to a particular age group. Do we have young people who feel the need for a group or program? The presence of a youth minister may be an important consideration for a young family. One thing to keep an eye on is the state of the new congregation. Someone making a move from one closing congregation may not want to go through the closure experience again. Who can blame them? It is appropriate to ask about the health of the congregation that a person is considering is joining.

One of the planning tasks faced by both the closure team and the congregation will be the future use of assets and resources. What kind of "legacy" will the congregation leave? Parishioners have to think about what life will look like once this closure is complete. What will life look like once the congregation "dies"? Where can a person find hope that a resurrection of some kind will be experienced? What kinds of new ministries will emerge and grow from this closing congregation? In addressing this issue of leaving a legacy of some sort, N. Nelson Grande Jr. writes, "Though not every congregation is fortunate enough to have valuable tangible assets to pass on, every congregation has a legacy to leave."[6] Every congregation has something to offer. It can be the proceeds from the sale of any property or it can be the gift of furniture or other artifacts that can help enrich the life of another congregation or new ministry of some sort. Parishioners may have thoughts about what will happen to the communion table and baptismal font. They may know of a new congregation in need of certain material things the closing congregation has on hand. There may be an existing program that can be transferred to a nearby congregation where it can continue to grow.

In discussing the dispersal of proceeds from the sale of any church building, a colleague of mine stressed the need to nurture new ministries. One resource on church closures agrees, and adds, "The congregation's resources could be used to form new communities of faith, either through the creation of a permanent fund for new congregational establishment or an outright gift."[7] There is an added suggestion in this same resource that "Maybe the congregation would like its resources to under gird the whole mission of the church." One possibility is to include the wider church when planning the dispersal of any assets. This is where the concept of tithing comes in. The traditional concept of tithing refers to the designation of a certain portion of our resources towards the work of the church or temple. In the case of a church closure we can dedicate certain percentage of the proceeds to the overall mission of a denomination. When a seed dies a new plant or tree is created. The possibility of creating and nourishing new life can inspire efforts to find innovative or unique ways of assigning the congregation's assets. Each denomination may have its own guidelines on how assets are dealt with.

The United Brethren, for example, have set guidelines for what happens when a congregation decides to close. In Chapter 26 of its "Discipline 2001-2005" it's noted that "When a decision is made (to close a church), the following actions will occur: a) All property will become the property of the annual conference. B) A letter will be sent to each member outlining possible options regarding church attendance and membership in nearby churches, information on what will happen to church property, and any other relevant information. C) Members shall transfer their membership to the local church of their choice. If that is not done within six months the conference superintendent may close the roll by removing the names from United Brethren membership".

It is important to pay strict attention to any documented rules that your respective denomination may have concerning church closures. The United Brethren guidelines raise a few important points—some of which we have already considered. Other denominations may have rules and guidelines that can help with our planning. Like the United Brethren, most denominations have manuals and handbooks that outline policies and procedures. The official manual of the United Church of Canada is another example of this kind of material. There are a series of items in this manual that apply to closures and how certain levels of church management should participate in the process. One of the main problems with many these manual sections are that they are vague. There are some gaps to be navigated and interpretations to be made in a manner that ensures that people and groups are treated fairly.

One example of a gap that came into play in one local closure was section 337 in the United Church of Canada Manual,[8] which states:

"Where, in the opinion of the Presbytery, the functioning of a pastoral charge is ineffectual, or where the Pastoral Charge requests the Presbytery to take action on its behalf, the Presbytery shall take adopt such measures as it may deem necessary."

This section raises a number of questions and issues. What constitutes "ineffectual" and what guidelines or standards are used as a yardstick? What kinds of "measures" are appropriate in a given situation? Who makes these important decisions? This was one of the debates around the situation involving my previous congregation. This can be a tricky judgment call. It's not something that can be taken lightly.

Another concern that can be raised about this manual section is the need to assess when the wider church has gone too far in responding to a troubling situation. There seems to be a fine, yet unwritten line that can be crossed and that very few people really know about. These kinds of uncertainties may leave a group feeling lost, or "out to sea". There may be some questions as to whether or not some decisions are legal. This is where a strong relationship with the denomination continues being helpful.

The wider denomination may be able to help us interpret the many facets of the rules and guidelines that help order our work as congregations and individuals. The United Church of Canada Manual sections such as 337, for example, stand in contrast with the sections on items like "appeals". These are important sections as they offer people a way to challenge decisions that they feel are inappropriate and premature. The sections dealing with appeals are laid out in legalistic detail. Again, we need to be aware of the fine line here. We also have to be aware of possible abuses. In clear-cut decisions antagonists may file appeals or complaints knowing full well that they will fail. It is simply their way of "getting back" at the people who supposedly have made their life difficult.

Regardless of whether these sections are vague or extremely legalistic, the reason that a denominational rulebook is so important is because of its legal value. If there are conflicts and disputes, the rulebook is something that can be used in processing these disagreements. It is also a resource that can come in handy for those disagreements that wind up in court. One of the questions that is usually asked is, "did you follow the rules?" It's important to carry this question with us as we go about our work.

Another reason why it is important to pay attention to legal requirements is with respect to property. One of the more practical questions when planning a church closure concerns the building and any other property in the congregation's possession. What happens to the building? How do we deal with a building that is filled with so many memories, where funerals, weddings, and worship services have been held, and where people have experienced growing relationships with God? It is tough to lock the door and walk away from these kinds of experiences. One of the things that I have heard a lot in my time at my previous congregation has been the comment that "I was married here". People spoke of funerals held for friends and family. Parents wanted their children to have some continuing tie with the congregation in which they were baptized. As we will be considering in future chapters, sentiment plays an important role in how we respond to church closures.

This sentiment is an important part of the planning process. We can be reminded that church buildings are sacred space and should be cared for accordingly. When a building is set-aside as a place where people worship and build community there are certain expectations that come as a result. Many of these expectations come out of our sense of the use for sacred spaces. We may develop certain standards that identify what we consider appropriate uses for a church building. We may be offended when these standards are compromised in any way.

In some denominations decisions around the use and possible disposal of a building is out of the local group's hands. So much depends on the people or groups who actually own the property. With one local property, for example, it is a denomination's area conference that makes the final decision. Different levels of denominational oversight and management may have their say but the ultimate decision remains at the regional, or in this case, conference level. People need to be informed as to how this decision-making process with respect to property will work. They need to know how much input they will be allowed. They will need time to consider the available possibilities. Is there a project or ministry that is being developed and in need of resources? Is there another congregation that will be the destination for many of the former members of the closing congregation?

People build intense relationships with the buildings in which their communities of faith are housed. Sometimes it is difficult to know what or whom a person is worshipping. Is a person worshipping God or simply attending there because they have a commitment to the bricks and mortar? These assets are "closely tied to people's most deeply rooted religious beliefs and cherished memories."[9] We face the challenge of reminding ourselves that even though important things have happened in a particular church building that does not mean that the property should always be a church. If a person has an experience of the holy in a certain spot that does not mean this location has to be permanently set-aside as a worship space. We can hold that place in our hearts but we must leave it at that and move on. In describing our relationship with church buildings John Webster Grant has written, "Although in times of affluence congregations seem to replace their buildings with little reluctance, they become strangely attached to them in times of stress."[10]

When a congregation is closed and a church building sold, the results can be troubling to the people who invested so much of their lives in these congregations. While we will be touching on grief in the next chapter it is an important consideration when we make plans for the building itself. Some church buildings are converted into housing or businesses. Some buildings are torn down completely so that some other kind of development can be built on the same spot. These are some of the hopes and dreams that can be discussed with the person chosen to list and sell the building and property. We have discussed the possibility that we will reach a point where a professional may need to be consulted. This is one of those times. Very few, if any, clergy and volunteers have the necessary training and credentials to properly list and sell property. There may be someone in a congregation with a real estate license of some sort but without the necessary training and experience with which to give the job "due diligence". Finding a real estate person who knows what they are doing with church property benefits everyone touched by the congregation's closure.

This notion of "due diligence" is one that I have learned through experience. To me, this simply means that we do our best in ensuring that all of our bases have been covered. In one case it was making the effort to ensure that any potentially interested groups were contacted so that they would have a chance to look at the building and make an offer if they wished. We also tried to show due diligence in securing a bid as close to the list price as possible. If the proceeds from a sale are going to be directed towards new ministries then it is important that we try to gather as much as possible from the sale. This effort to sell the building for as close to list price as possible needs to be balanced with the intended use of the building by the purchaser.

When we were trying to sell the building owned by my

previous congregation one of the interested parties wanted to convert the building into an auction house. This possibility hinted of "letting the money traders into the temple" and it was a troubling thought for many. Another group was considering the development of an arts and cultural facility. Historically, church buildings have been converted into art galleries, libraries, schools and other kinds of educational facilities. One of the considerations when looking at these kinds of uses is whether or not the building is accessible to people with physical challenges.

There was one church that was converted into a roller rink[11] and one can only imagine how former parishioners felt about that situation. Parishioners will have strong feelings about what will become of the church buildings and these should be considered when examining the different options for future use. Any future use of the building may help determine the level of grief that people may experience. A church building used to house a new congregation may be well received compared with the possible construction of a condo project.

For congregations meeting in smaller wooden buildings there is always the possibility of moving their buildings somewhere else. Is there a rural community in which a small group of people is looking to begin a new ministry? Is there a piece of land in a new area where the demographics are more favorable for a renewed congregation?

In a recent issue of The United Church Observer there was a brief article and picture concerning the move of an unused church building.[12] The congregation has ceased using this 129-year-old structure and there were limited options considering the fact there was no electricity or heat. The church building was sold to a nearby "living history museum" for one dollar. The effort to move this building to its new home was a considerable one. The move was tricky as it involved both traveling by road and water. A tremendous amount of equipment was involved, including both a flat bed truck and a barge. The effort seemed to be worth it, however, as there would be a new lease on life for the building that had been an important part of so many lives. The people having oversight of the building wanted to continue its presence and service in the area. The move to the museum would meet these needs and also affect thousands of people interested in maintaining an important connection with the local Gaelic culture and history.

People seem more at ease when we try to assure them that every effort will be made to ensure that the building in which they have invested so much time, energy, and financial resources into will remain a church. Jennifer Lynn Baskerville writes, "As a congregation grieves for what is no longer, members may find it helpful and appropriate to remember and grieve for the building as well."[13]

As we continue our discussion about what to do with the building we can be reminded that when we close the doors of the church for the last time we do not lock God inside when we leave. God cannot be locked inside a box or a building. God is too big for that. Throughout history people have tried to build cabins and provide tents in which God could live. God continues to remind us that this is not how things work. God's habitation needs extends beyond buildings, bricks and mortar. God goes with us as we continue our spiritual journeys. God is our companion and not the building's.

There are some technical issues that need to be raised here when talking about the future use of the church building. One of the things that need to be examined is the legal paper work around who actually owns the property. We have talked about the importance of tracking legal documents in the previous chapter. There may be other questions around where the deed is kept, and so on. Is there a mortgage that needs to be dealt with? What are the contractual obligations? There were a number of groups who were using the church building when my previous congregation closed. The church secretary contacted each one to confirm what our commitments were to them. There was another congregation also meeting in the building and our commitments to them had to be considered until decisions were made by the new owners of the building and their wishes for the future use of the facility. Another consideration when selling the building is the question of what to do with any weddings or other events that have been booked at the church? In my previous congregation the office manager and I made the decision to include any outstanding wedding dates as conditions in any sale offer. This may be a problem for congregations with a high number of bookings. It may be helpful to find more creative ways of accommodating these types of commitments.

Another concern that will be a part of the planning process is membership. Decisions have to be made around whether or not there will be baptisms. What happens when people ask to join the congregation through confirmation or transfer? It is not a good idea to transfer members in from other congregations when a church is closing as this sends the wrong message. It may suggest that there is still a chance to reverse any of the closure decisions. Politely and firmly insist that no incoming transfers can be accepted as the congregation is closing.

There can be baptisms and confirmation where pastoral concerns call for this kind of action. When my previous congregation was closing we had a number of requests for baptism from parishioners who wanted themselves or their children baptized. Setting appropriate limits for these baptisms can be something accomplished by both the congregation and the closure team.

Throughout this chapter we have been talking about buildings, assets, and membership records. As we make our way through this planning process, however, it becomes all too easy to become obsessed with numbers. Abraham Heschel has written, "The problem is not to boost the numbers but inspire the hearts."[14] In other words, there is a time for evangelism and spreading the Gospel. There is also a time to care for people and be with them in the changes that they are facing. It's this kind of pastoral care that we will consider in Chapter Five.

One loose end that may escape the attention of many is the question of what to do with the records a congregation accumulates over the years. Records are often stored in out of the way places and could be easily forgotten. This may seem trivial but there is a real historic value to this kind of paperwork. There are registers and files that have been kept for historical and legal reasons. These are items that have contributed to the history and tradition of a congregation and will help preserve the congregation's story for generations. It is for this reason that they have to be treated with love and respect.

One of the possibilities in dealing with records is their transmission to any archives that exist within a region or a denomination. Denominations tend to have historical or archives committees with the experience and knowledge to deal with the kind of documentation that a congregation accumulates. With regard to transmitting records to an archive of one type or other Paul Daniels writes, "While on one level this represents good record keeping practices, on a deeper level, obvious to those people whose church is closing, such ritual action is the very real passing on of the vehicles of memory to safekeeping in the new setting."[15]

The closure team that we have been talking about can be an effective source of information concerning the transmission of important records. They can make whatever contacts are necessary to ensure a smooth transmission. If there are people on this team with this kind of knowledge then that is an advantage. Educational opportunities can also be provided for those team members interested in learning more about records and archives. I make this suggestion because of the importance of organizing and creating an inventory of any available files and records. This kind of effort is important as the archives may have their own requirements in terms of what is sent to them from a congregation.[16]

When we talk about records and files we can also address the existence of any published congregational histories. One local congregation had published such a history and had a number of copies available when the decision was made to close. What were they going to do with the remaining copies? At least one copy should be sent to the respective denomination's archives. A local museum may also be interested in receiving a copy. Perhaps the best option is to give remaining copies of the congregation's history to members and any other interested persons. They would make great souvenirs and mementos for parishioners. Media representatives may find them valuable resources when working on a story. There are many possibilities.

In talking about distributing things we can discuss the need to deal with any photographs, artwork or other gifts that remain with the congregation. It may be a good idea to contact local museums and ask what they would be looking for in terms of materials for display. When it comes to photographs there are two possible ways of dealing with them. When my previous congregation closed we created a photo display for the final tea. People were asked to review the display and if they wished, take whatever picture was meaningful to them. The remaining photos were transmitted to archives along with the records.

There may also be other kinds of gifts or artifacts that have become a part of the congregation. A family may have donated a communion table, for example. When the congregation decides to close there may be an effort to contact this family to see what their wishes would be for this important piece of furniture. Do they want the table back or would they want it to be sent to another congregation? Families whose gifts are unrecorded may come forward to either reclaim their gift or suggest a new recipient. As we have already stated, these kinds of things would be a wonderful gift to any new congregation being started within the community or the denomination itself.

When discussing the gifts that can be offered to other congregations we can also consider the reality of departing staff. How will these kinds of departures be handled? Will the denomination be responsible for placing staff in new situations? Will clergy and others be responsible for finding their own employment? There will have to be extensive consultation with denominational authorities on how to handle layoffs and severance packages. There may also be labour laws and required paperwork to be considered. Closing a congregation is hard and difficult work and this fact should be considered when preparing severance packages that are offered to staff.

A friend of mine was hired to manage the closure a local factory. Part of her two-year contract ensured a six-month payout at the completion of her commitment. This would provide the financial resources to carry her over until she could find a new job. This package also helped provide time in which she could recover from the difficult challenge.

Financial resources can be provided for these packages from the sale of any congregational property. The actual numbers can be negotiated with denominational officials. The thing to keep in mind when determining the final numbers is that these packages have to be fair. We have to consider the time invested by staff in the congregation. We can also consider the potential for a person's ability to find work in similar fields. In many professions it is a practice to offer one month's severance for every year served. There may be contractual obligations requiring attention. Treating staff fairly is important in any planning process.

Good planning is an important part of any effort to close a congregation. Good planning minimizes the potential for conflict[17] and releases energy for ministry and caring. We will be talking about the importance of caring for one another in chapters four and five.

Chapter Three Checklist

- Who is responsible for planning the congregation's closure? Who will be helping the planners from the congregation's denomination?
- Is there a plan for communicating with the media?
- Who will be making arrangements for pastoral care? What are the roles of the clergy leaders and the board, for example? What can each parishioner do to help with the closure process?
- What will be done with the building, furniture and other assets? Are there any financial assets that will need to be found and dealt with? Who will be arranging for the realtors, auditors, etc?
- Who will be planning the final service and any other related activities?
- What can the closure team contribute to this planning process?
- Who will ensure that archives and records are handled properly?

Endnotes

1. Kramer, Kenneth "The Sacred Art of Dying: How World Religions Understand Death" (Mahwah, 1988), p.201
2. Auger, p.97
3. Whalley, Lawrence "The Aging Brain" (New York, 2001), p.67
4. Kuhl, P.27
5. Robertson, P.202ff
6. Ending With Hope, P.63
7. "Is It Time To Fold the Tent?", P.7
8. United Church of Canada Manual, 2001 Edition
9. New Brunswick Reader, June 15th, 2003 p.6

10. Grant, John Webster "George Pidgeon: A Biography" (Toronto, 1962), p.99
11. New Brunswick Reader, P.8
12. United Church Observer, January 2004, p.8
13. Ending With Hope, P. 159
14. Heschel, P.103
15. Ending With Hope, P. 148
16. A suggested checklist is on P. 153 of "Ending With Hope".
17. Haugk, p.94

Chapter Four
Grief

A number of years ago Resurrection United Methodist church was planted in the southwest area of Little Rock Arkansas. It was created to minister to the needs of African American people living in this section of the state capital. Over the years the congregation had met in a variety of rented locations with clergy serving in both full and part time capacities. After numerous efforts to create a vibrant ministry denominational officials made the decision to close and seek a new way of ministering to the community. Despite continuing efforts to develop and redevelop the ministry, people in the congregation still felt a series of strong emotions when they found out about the decision to close. There were signs that things were not working out as people had hoped. There were efforts to try and figure out what has going on. And yet people still felt a sense of devastation and even betrayal, when hearing the news.[1]

Our response to news that our congregation is closing can be like a scene out of a western movie. There is often that spot in the movie when someone bursts out of a bank shouting something like "We wuz robbed!" Feeling "robbed" is one of the many responses to the losses we experience in life. This is what bereavement is all about. People and things leave us and we are left to remember and rebuild our lives. When a congregation closes people can experience a sense of loss. We may experience intense emotions that affect how we see the church, the denomination, and perhaps even the world around us. We may lose touch with people with whom we have worshipped and served. We may lose a sense of community and belonging. We may feel powerless in the face of decisions made by an organization bigger than ourselves. We may also lose a sense of place and contribution that has been an important part of our lives. In experiencing this loss we go through a time of grief.

Loss is something we can often experience. Even the most trivial losses can profoundly affect us. A number of years ago columnist Daphne Merkin lost a scarf in a New York City taxi cab. Merkin tried to chase this cab several blocks before giving up and returning to a friend she had abandon a short distance away. In reflecting on this seemingly trivial happening Merkin writes, "What this has to do with is loss, the disappearance of anything—big or little, inanimate or human—that helps moor us in what George Eliot in Middlemarch called 'the largeness of the world.' To grieve over a loss is to grieve all losses." Merkin goes on to observe, "If I could undo this one loss, even if I had to die in the process, I could undo all the losses I'd suffered."[2]

We grieve many losses in life. These losses seem to come together, forming some sort of knot that stays with us as we make our way through life. We can grieve the loss of something as simple as a scarf. We can also grieve the loss of a close friend or family member. Grief is also a primary consideration in the closing of a congregation and will be further discussed in this chapter. When it comes to grief there has been a tremendous amount of information published over the past fifty years or so. There has been excellent work done in the area of loss and bereavement and some of these resources appear in the bibliography at the end of this book. I will be touching on some of this published material as it applies to church closures. Some of the information will be helpful in understanding people's experience as they face the loss of their faith communities and what this means for their lives.

None of us can go through life without some experience with grief. Colin Murray-Parkes names the reality of grief in all of our lives when he writes, "The pain of grief is just as much a part of life as the joy of love; it is, perhaps, the price we pay for love, the cost of commitment."[3] Murray-Parkes adds, "A bereaved person reacts to both loss and deprivation."[4] This can be true of the loss of a congregation. This sense of "loss" and "deprivation" can affect the level of intensity of the grief we experience. We can see some of this when Murray-Parkes writes, "...individuals are forced to give up one mode of life and accept another." When a congregation closes a person is forced to give up one community of faith and move on to another. Parishioners are forced to surrender cherished routines and relationships. These can be difficult changes and people will react to these changes in different ways. Some will resist while others will move on and try to establish a connection with a new congregation.

Grief is such a primal part of who we are as humans and it affects how we express ourselves in our community and relationships. This has been recorded through the years in both prose and poetry. From the ancient Greeks to many of our contemporary writers, there have been constant references to the importance and effort of expressing our losses and grief. The late Canadian thinker Northrop Frye has written, "This story of loss and regaining identity is...the framework of all literature."[5] In "Writing Grief" Christian Riegel suggests, "For grieving to be effective, the emotions of loss must be translated into words and must be articulated."[6] "Must" is an important word here as all too often we seem tempted to avoid dealing with the loss we experience in life. We may interpret some of the losses we experience as being small and somehow inconsequential. Jacques Derrida identifies the importance and reality of grief and mourning when he writes, "One should not develop a taste for mourning, yet mourn we *must*."[7]

Again, this word "must" is important when we remember that none of us can go through life without being touched by loss. There are times when we are thrown out of paradise, so to speak. There are times when we are faced with a dry, lifeless wilderness in which we confront the challenge of finding our way out again. It is like falling into a deep hole and having to claw our way out. We face a time for reflection and remembering. We also face a time of rebuilding and reconnecting. Carolyn Pogue writes, "Unless we take the time to consider our losses and readjust to life, how we can fully embrace the joy of being alive. Since death is a part of life."[8]

When dealing with grief Jeanette Auger writes, "Grief represents the emotional, physical, and sociocultural reactions that we experience due to loss." Auger goes on to list the kinds of losses that can lead us to experience grief. These losses can include the death of a friend or loved one, a job or a possession. We can add the closing of a congregation to this list. This is one of the reasons why I feel that it is important to consider grief as a reality in any work of closing a congregation. It's important to include something about grief in any resource dealing with these kinds of closure. We cannot ignore grief. We cannot bury it. Grief is something that affects every part of us. Grief is something that can affect us physically, psychologically, socially and spiritually. Auger writes, any loss is "a deeply distressful event which challenges our ability to cope with everyday life, and causes us to question who we are without the missing person, object, pet or event."[9]

I remember visiting my grandparents' house for Sunday dinner and the pressure cooker would be on the stove. As the temperature of the contents increased, the pressure built to a point where the steam would need to escape. If the steam was not released then the pressure would blow the lid off. I often wondered what would happen if someone forgot about this pressure cooker on the stove. I often tried to imagine the mess we would have if all of the contents of the pot were blown across the room. A similar thing can happen to us. If we cannot find a way of managing the emotional energy that builds at a time like this then we face some serious consequences in the long run. These consequences can be anything from psychological to physical ailments. Auger refers to the potential for the experience of physical pain when we face a time of grief. In response to this possibility Colin Murray-Parkes writes, "Grief may not produce physical pain, but it is very unpleasant and usually disturbs function."[10]

One of the ways we begin to lower the pressure, so to speak, and deal with the reality of loss is by talking. Talking about death and grief does not have to be a morbid conversation. It is a conversation that can happen at almost any time in life. Auger writes, "To be concerned with death and its celebration is not 'morbid'. It is proper to reflect on the certainty of life. All healthy and vigorous civilizations of the past have apprehended the significance of death."[11] While conversations about death are necessary, they are not always easy. Abraham Heschel claims that the subject is "strange and totally inaccessible."[12] It seems beyond our ability to understand. This makes grief all the more difficult and complicated. This makes conversation and communication all the more important.

The conversation around death and loss is important for when churches close as well. Church closures bring endings out into the open in a way that cannot be ignored. In having this conversation we can sort out our own thoughts and beliefs on what death means for us. We can think about endings and new beginnings in a way that can touch our entire lives. "We avoid death because it reminds us of our own mortality"[13] N. Nelson Granade adds that people "like to visit newborn babies in the hospital, but few want to venture into the oncology ward". This avoidance of death could be a factor in how people respond to the news that their congregation is closing.

When we examine the grief journey we may experience the temptation to rely on the stages identified by Elizabeth Kubler-Ross. In discussing the realities of death and dying Kubler-Ross names the stages of "Denial", "Bargaining", "Anger", "Depression", and "Acceptance". These steps have been accepted in many circles and disciplines. In critiquing Kubler-Ross' work Heather Robertson writes, "To their dismay, doctors and nurses who tried to move their patients through Kubler-Ross's five stages discovered that her theory didn't work."[14] We do not grieve by moving through stages in an orderly way. If we were to look at a series of points labeled A to E and then plot our experience of grief, we would see a line that was bouncing all over the place. We would be tracing a line that would go from A to C and then back to B. There is the possibility that we would be returning to the same spots over and over again.

One of the helpful things about identifying stages is that we see some of the realities that we face when grieving. There are times when we pass through shock and denial. There are times when we get angry and sad. We may reach a point when we feel that we have accepted the situation and then experience something that sends us back to anger or depression. It could be a word or gesture that stirs something within us that almost forces us to relive the grief. We may be walking through a mall and hear a song that reminds us of the one who has died. We may smell something that touches a familiar chord. We may be worshipping with a new congregation when we hear a hymn that takes us back to a previous encounter or experience. Whenever I hear the hymn "Holy, Holy, Holy", for example, I am taken back to the congregation in which I worshipped as a child. We always began our services with this hymn and the memory endures to this day. People worshipping in their new congregation may experience a similar sensation when they share in a particular prayer or hymn. When we try and keep track of our grieving it may be difficult to see any kind of pattern. It may seem as if we're moving in circles. This is one of the realities of grief.

Perhaps the first response to grief is the experience of shock and disbelief. One Saturday morning after arriving at a new congregation the phone rang. It was a friend of ours who was living in another town at the time. Her husband had died in a farming accident the night before and she was phoning us with the news. When we hung up the phone my spouse and I just looked at each other in utter disbelief. We couldn't find anything to say. David Kuhl talks about this kind of silence. He writes, "Death comes, and, with it silence, a permanent, implacable type of silence."[15] This shock and numbness is a beginning in the grief and bereavement process.

Virginia Ironside also talks about shock in her book "You'll Get Over It". She describes this moment as, "...white-faced disbelief, a light headed sense of unreality, a stunned feeling as thought you had been hit over the head with a hammer."[16] This kind of shock is difficult to describe. People can experience added symptoms like exhaustion. We may feel numb and yet also calm. This experience of numbness may result from the overload that a bereaved person experiences. It may also be the result of surprise.

One of the feelings that may complicate the experience of shock is that of "relief". We may feel relieved when a person whom we believe to have been suffering finally lets go and dies. We may see it as some sort of blessing that the pain and suffering is now over. I watched as some of this relief was shown when the wider church stepped in and closed a local congregation that had been experiencing a traumatic closure process. The arguing and bickering were now over. It was time to grieve and mourn in an effort to move on. Relief is something many people experience, especially when they have witnessed stress and suffering within the life of an individual or institution.

Historically, an early response to grief has been identified as being "denial". We have often thought of denial as being something negative. We may find ourselves trying to move people through this experience as soon as possible. Heather Robertson suggests an alternative interpretation and explains that denial is "a normal defense mechanism."[17] She describes it as something that "can buy people time to pull themselves together." She goes on to write, "Unless denial threatens to harm others ... the inability to hear bad news may be a better way of coping than depression."[18] Denial offers us the opportunity to let the seriousness of the situation sink in. We cannot force a person to deal with any kind of tragic news all at once. They need to take some time to think about what they have heard.

Another aspect of grief is "bargaining". When a person hears of a terminal diagnosis there may be an effort to make changes so that the outcome will be somehow altered. There may be an effort to "buy more time" or find a miracle cure that can help change the situation. A person may reason that if they quit smoking or change their diet then the progress of their condition will somehow change and they will extend their available time. Many patients will consult with practitioners of alternative medicine. Some of these efforts are extremely risky and don't always achieve the results we would hope for.

This act of bargaining can also happen in congregations. Tanya Stormo Rasmussen states that it is not unusual for bargaining to happen when a congregation decides to close.[19] People will want another chance and will often become desperate in their efforts to secure the necessary time to work a miracle. This may be complicated by feelings of frustration that more hasn't been done to help keep the congregation open. People may feel that if they begin doing the right things then everything will return to "normal" and all will be well. Congregations may also experience the temptation to rush into hasty decisions around options such as clustering and amalgamations. These possibilities should have already been carefully considered before the decision to close was reached.

When a local congregation was making the decision to close a meeting was called in which to bring the matter to a vote. At this meeting the question was raised about whether or not the decision could be reversed. The representative from their denomination offered his opinion that any decision could be reversed if any new evidence came to people's attention. This opinion is supported by parliamentary procedure in that any vote can be reversed under certain circumstances. Within the context of the meeting this comment was accurate. There was a period of time in which this comment would continue to be accurate. This period of time was all too brief, however.

People in the congregation took this one comment and began using it long after it had lost its effectiveness. Normally a decision cannot be reversed once action by the wider church has been taken. In this congregation's case the denomination began approving requests and passing motions in support of the congregation's request to close. Late in the proceedings an outside group approached the congregation claiming to have a plan and resources but even then it would have been difficult to change the decision. We'll speak more about this group's efforts in a later chapter but some of this story will be important as we deal with the bargaining stage.

Some of the active members in this congregation used the earlier comment by the denominational representative as a kind of bargaining chip in an effort to get the congregational decision reversed. This comment was raised whenever people wanted to revisit the main decision to close. Even though the situation had passed the point where the decision could legally be reversed these words were constantly offered as a representative's opinion that carried weight in the overall process.

There are many other ways in which a group can bargain. They can bargain for more time or they can try to convince people that the decision to close has been a wrong one. People may want more time to wait for a miracle to happen and return the congregation to its former health. People in the congregation were told that if there were a huge donation or increase in attendance then the wider church would reconsider its decision. Again, while there is some accuracy to this kind of statement it is not always helpful to vocalize it. We have to be careful about what we say at all times. It can come back to haunt us and perhaps cause an increasing amount of damage in the long run. It's probably best to stay with the technical process itself and avoid any kind of speculation. There are times when it is best to be silent.

When dealing with the different aspects of grief we can also consider the realities of "yearning", "pining" and "protest". These aspects can be a part of an overall searching process. Murray-Parkes suggests, "Pining is the subjective and emotional component of the urge to search that is shown by many species of social animal."[20] When my spouse and I were visiting family on Vancouver Island we set out on a day trip, and we left our pet dog, Rosie, at the house. There were a couple of people remaining at the house so we didn't worry about leaving Rosie with them. When we had left, however, Rosie found an open door and attempted to follow us. When my father-in-law saw her she was sniffing her way down the long driveway in search of us. This searching seems to be an instinct that we, as humans, experience as well. Intellectually, we know that there is often little point in searching. There seems to be another part of us, however, that finds this reality difficult to accept. We know where the church building is and we can easily find out the necessary information concerning the congregation's closure. Our instincts respond in a different way, however. Murray-Parkes writes, "this does not prevent them from experiencing a strong impulse to search."[21]

"Searching" is an important, and instinctive part of the grief journey. We also seem inclined to protest. The Roman Catholic Archdiocese of Boston closed St. Mary's due to a shortage of priests. This closure left 350 members to find new congregations. Every afternoon at about the same time Anna Della Monica would begin her personal vigil outside St. Mary's Roman Catholic Church. Anna is the former organist at St. Mary's and sees this protest as a way of communicating her feelings about what has happened to her spiritual home. She sees it as her own way of sending a message. She begins her protest by wrapping a piece of black plastic around a pillar of the church building and then carries a sign. "It shows how I feel, and I don't like it." she said.[22] This is simply one example of what pining and protest can look like.

Another word that we can use to describe this kind of searching and protest is "lament". A lament is a cry of anguish and pain. It can also be a cry of frustration that emerges from a sense of being powerless, and helpless. It's one of the ways in which we vocalize our grief and sorrow. We can see many examples in the Bible and there is even an entire book set aside within one of the testaments for this kind of writing. Heather Robertson perhaps states this kind of feeling most accurately when she writes, "If I were facing immanent death, I'd find keening and raging more appropriate than brooding over my past, performing a list of tasks, or composing myself, like John Donne, into a corpse-to-be."[23] This protest can contribute to the conflict we discuss in Chapter Six.

Murray-Parkes identifies other aspects of grief that will also be important for our consideration here. He talks about the presence of "bitterness", "resistance", and "blaming."[24] These three things can also be related to many of the other stages of grieving we have been addressing to this point in our discussion. For our purposes here we can simply name them and talk about their contribution to the overall grief journey.

In talking about bitterness, resistance and blaming we can

also discuss the presence and reality of anger when we grieve. All of these components contribute to the building emotional pressure that can be experienced within each one of us. Whether we want to admit it or not anger is something we all experience in life. The writer of Ephesians 4:26 deals with the reality of anger by advising, "Be angry, but do not sin." Anger is a reality in our lives and how we deal with it is important. How do we deal with all of the emotional energy that is generated when we are angry? How do we manage all of this energy in a way that doesn't hurt anyone, including ourselves? Anger is something we need to deal with constructively. When we bury our anger we risk depression.[25] We also risk releasing this anger in ways that are inappropriate and wind up causing pain and harm.

Anger is something that can surprise us. Virginia Ironside writes, "how easy it is for an angry bereaved person to take offense from even the most sympathetic words and actions."[26] This is one of the reasons why many funeral directors speak in such hushed tones. One director has told me that he is never the one to crack a joke when helping families make funeral arrangements. If a family is laughing and joking about something then he simply lets them be. This can be one of the ways they can be dealing with their loss. Emotions can change all too quickly, however. It doesn't seem to take much to make the emotional jump from laughter to rage. In speaking about the presence of anger Dylan Thomas seems to be on to something when, in his poem "Do Not Go Gentle Into That Good Night", he tells us to "rage against the dying of the light".

This experience of anger and rage is present when a congregation closes. It's not so much a question of the entire group being angry over an extended period of time. It's something that emerges from time to time. This is what makes dealing with grief and conflict so difficult and unpredictable. We are dealing with a group of people who can become angry at any time. We may find ourselves "walking on eggshells", so to speak, in an effort to avoid triggering a hostile reaction to something we say or do. A lot of this anger and rage may come out of a sense of being both powerless and helpless in the face of events. Things may be happening that seem beyond our control. We may even experience anger with ourselves for not having done more to reverse the situation and save the congregation.

I was the target of people's anger when it was perceived that I was not doing enough to work with groups wanting to rescue my previous congregation and reverse the decision to close. Even though these kinds of efforts would have undermined the democratic decision of both the members of the congregation and the denomination, some people seemed to think that I should have made the effort any way. These kinds of conflicting expectations place staff, people, and other leaders in a potentially unstable situation.

When expressing anger we may be trying to get rid of some of that emotional energy. We may not know where to focus it, however, so we take advantage of people who become "targets of opportunity". Targets of opportunity can be people who say or do something that act as a trigger inside of others who then make the choice to unload their anger and rage on the targets. We all make choices around how we deal with anger. When we take advantage of targets of opportunity we may think we are doing this to protect family, friends or ourselves. Regardless of our motivations, clergy are one of the most common targets simply because of their availability. It's also easier to blame the minister for something than it is to take out our rage on a friend or relative, or accept responsibility ourselves. Virginia Ironside writes, "Rage is a pretty anti-social emotion at the best of times, even when it is directed against deserving targets."[27] This complicates the process when we proceed with important meetings and decisions. We'll be talking more about this when we deal with conflict in an upcoming chapter.

In dealing with the reality of anger and rage we can

also confront our anger with God. As with any intimate relationship we can confront the challenge of finding healthy ways of expressing our anger. What is a healthy way of expressing our anger at God? What is a healthy way of focusing and dissipating the emotional energy so that we can work at difficult questions and confront the roadblocks that keep us from continuing our relationship with God?

One of these roadblocks people experience when they grieve is despair. Tanya Stormo Rasmussen writes, "The despair that some members may experience may manifest itself in any number of ways."[28] We may experience depression. We may also experience a profound sadness. Virginia Ironside writes, "Most painful feelings stem from real feelings of sadness."[29] Ironside goes on to add, "Sadness and misery may strike at any time." We may experience this sadness for some surprising reasons such as at the closing of the church because of missed opportunities. We mourn the gaps and silence that will be in our lives. We mourn the lost relationships and involvement. We may find ourselves wondering about the future of the friendships we have developed. We may ask about future possibilities of building relationships and community. How will we invest our time and energy? Who is going to care for us in time of crisis and concern?

Sadness is a reality that we will face and it is more than appropriate to express this emotion. In the act of crying and shedding tears we relieve the power and energy of this sadness. We release the emotional energy so that we can move on. Sometimes we cannot move on. We may get lost in the crying and find it difficult to find our way out. We need to be careful in that there are different kinds of tears. Ironside writes, "Certainly a good cry can make everything temporarily alright, but tears are not an end in themselves. After all, some people ... get stuck in their grief and just go on crying and crying... Perhaps it's the different type of tears that are important." Ironside identifies some of the possibilities when she writes, "According to some psychologists, there are different types of crying: shallow weeping and deep weeping."[30] These different levels describe the intensity of emotions we face when we grieve.

Without a detailed awareness of where we are in the grief process we may feel as if we are simply moving in circles. When we speak of "moving in circles" we introduce the potential for an experience of the feeling of futility. We may find ourselves asking, "What's the use?" Canadian military psychiatrists have discovered that futility was one of the experiences leading to something called "combat fatigue", or "Battle Exhaustion", during the Second World War.[31] Julia Kristeva expresses this more precisely when she writes, "when all escape routes are blocked, animals as well as men learn to withdraw rather than flee or fight."[32]

This sense of futility can lead to the onset of depression. Speed Leas writes, "...one of the causes of depression is the belief that action is futile."[33] When we find our car in mud or on ice we may wind up spinning our tires in an effort to get back to solid ground. We keep pressing the accelerator in an effort to increase the speed of the tires thinking that this may help. When we realize that this is not going to work we may get frustrated and angry. We may also become sad and feel powerless to control anything happening around us.

Moving out of this depression will take a lot of work. When we realize that spinning our tires is not going to get us out of the mud we have to find another way of freeing our vehicle. We may have to grab a shovel and begin digging ourselves out. We may be able to ask someone to come to our assistance with a tow truck or give us a push. We can move out of our depression by examining our lives to find out what is contributing to our experience of sadness and we can also consider our options. We can also try and find out what it will take to improve our mood. It may simply be a case of finding someone with whom we can share our experiences and feelings. We can approach any of the closure team assigned to work with our congregation. We may be able to phone one of the pastoral care people asked to share in the same work. It may be something as simple as meeting with a friend for coffee or a movie. There is always the possibility the depression is serious enough that we require a visit to the doctor and a possible prescription for anti-depressants.

With regards to depression that emerges from the closure of a congregation, we can consider something that Speed Leas has written in his work on church leadership and conflict. In "Leadership and Conflict" Leas writes, "There are four things that a leaders often do to alleviate these feelings of powerlessness: create success experiences; help only when asked; encourage collaboration, and reward, rather than punish."[34] In a previous chapter we talked about the legacy, which a congregation can leave a denomination or a ministry. A "success experience" may be the completion of congregational affairs in a way that shows people that the memory, and story of the congregation will live on in some new and hopeful way. Parishioners can do much of this work themselves. There may be times when help can be invited from outside but their active contribution to the work of creating a legacy can help reduce the chance of depression. When outside people and groups are invited to share in the work of closing a church this does not always have to be considered a negative thing. We all face times when we have done what we can in a situation and require someone's assistance in finishing the job. Moving from one home to another, for example, is difficult without assistance from family, friends or professional movers. There are times when we will have to ask for help and there is nothing wrong with that.

When we move through grief we may find ourselves reaching a stage we have come to call "acceptance". It may be difficult to understand the meaning of "acceptance". Are we at peace with the loss we have experienced? Have we let go and moved on? Have we reached some sort of spiritual plateau by which we can carry on with our life journeys? Is it really the end of the grief process? Is it really the beginning of something new? John Morgan writes, "The Buddhists teach us that the acceptance of the fact of loss is the beginning of spirituality."[35] In terms of the Christian congregation Ezra Earl Jones writes, "Perhaps an increasing number of congregations in the future will find it possible to celebrate their church's past ministry and fulfilled goals and accept the disbanding of the congregation as the completion of a job well done, rather than as a failure that produces guilt."[36]

Acceptance can be seen as a new beginning. We have come to grips with the loss we have experienced. We have remembered and offered thanks. We have reflected on what this loss has meant for us. We have also made some effort to rebuild our lives in response to the particular loss that we have faced. This certainly doesn't mean that we are finished, however. The memory of a person, for example, can live with us for as long as we live. We can carry these memories and stories with us as we make our way into whatever future lay ahead. In considering this kind of rebuilding, Jeanette Auger writes, "When people are able to move through their own unique grief process, however long that may take, eventually they come to a place of reestablishing their lives by accepting the loss of the deceased and incorporating memories of the deceased into a new life without them."[37]

We cannot complete any discussion on a complicated process like grief without including something about fear. Fear is simply a response to the unknown. We don't know what those noises are under the bed or in the backyard so we experience a physical response that prepares us for anything. Virginia Ironside writes, "Fear is one of the biggest emotions after a bereavement."[38] Ironside adds, "Why are we frightened of death? We are terrified of the unknown, we are terrified of how we may feel when someone dies—lost, lonely and bereft; we are terrified to think that we might die ourselves."[39] The closure of a congregation may be difficult as it may remind us of our own mortality. It may remind us of some of the realities faced by all living beings. One of the things that we may fear is abandonment. We may be afraid that friends and acquaintances will move on without us. We may be afraid that God will somehow forget us and leave us alone.

There are a few ways in which we can make our way through the fear and transition. We have already discussed the benefits of simply talking with a friend or clergyperson about what is happening. Another simple response can be the simple act of putting our experiences in writing. We can begin a journal in which we name, and track our feelings and identify our thoughts. We can outline the events and happenings that led up to the decision and work of closing the congregation. We can write about the importance that the congregation has had for us. We can talk about the good times. We can talk about the pain and the conflict. We can talk about the anger and the disappointment. There will be questions that can be asked and a search for answers engaged. We can express our feelings about people and groups in a place that is safe and confidential. We can even consider the hand that God has had in what has been going on. We can let off steam in a way that does not damage relationships and efforts in any way. We can pour our hearts out in safety.

While keeping a journal is important we can also deal with our grief by writing letters. We can focus our individual thoughts and feelings towards people by putting them on paper. This may be helpful when we are dealing with denominational officials who are not always available to hear our thoughts and feelings. It is always best to resist the temptation of actually mailing any of these letters. I have personally mailed several letters that were written in anger and have regretted my actions to this day. The simple act of writing, alone, may be enough to help us without actually sending these letters and causing trouble for ourselves down the road. It's usually a good idea to simply write the letter and then put it away in a safe place. It may also be a good idea to have a paper shredder nearby!

Our efforts to write about our experience with a closing church are an important part of the storytelling process. Story telling may be a way of helping the people of a congregation tap into their grief. Shakespeare once wrote, "Give sorrow words, the grief that does not speak knits the overwrought heart and bids it break."[40] Sharing our story gives us the opportunity to put our experiences into words and tap into the pain that can quickly become a burden.

When it comes to dealing with our grief, there can also be an effort to maintain existing relationships and make connections with a new congregation. We can arrange times when we can be with friends from the previous congregations. We can meet for meals and activities. We can invest time and energy into maintaining the connections we have valued through the years.

We can also seek out possible connections with people in the congregation we are joining. A person may reach a point when they will experience a need to find a new congregation. Auger calls this grief stage "reconnecting"[41]. This act of reconnecting is something in which clergy and lay leaders can assist. While I was serving a previous congregation a nearby church within our denomination closed. I received a list in the mail naming selected parishioners from this closing congregation who lived near my congregation. I was being asked to make contact with each of these people and invite them to visit and, perhaps, begin attending the congregation I was serving at the time. This effort to divide a list of people by geographic area seemed cold to me. Had anyone asked these folks where they wanted to go? Had anyone discussed the possibilities with the affected people?

People should be offered the opportunity of speaking with their minister or some other person so that they can discuss any plans of moving to another congregation. People should be encouraged to find someone to speak with who is recommended by people in the congregation, the wider community or by the wider denomination. When the minister knows the destination of a given parishioner, efforts can be made to contact clergy and lay people in the new congregation. These folks can be welcomed with a card, letter, note, or a phone call from clergy and lay people. Each congregation may have its own way of welcoming, introducing and including newcomers.

When making a referral we may have to go beyond denominational walls. This may be a reality in a rural area where denominations may only have congregations beyond the geographical reach of "orphaned" parishioners. There may be agreements developed between denominations to ensure that some sort of ministry is offered to the people of a closing congregation. These agreements are not unusual. When examining church history we can see where a number of pioneer communities saw denominations cooperate in building a local congregation. In the previous chapter I raised some important questions that can be asked when considering a new congregation. We can ask these same questions here. This will help the reconnecting process and help us in the continuing task of dealing with grief. It may be a helpful way of caring for people as they go through all of the different aspects of the grief process.

The experience of grief over a closing congregation may invite thoughts and feelings about a previous death or some other significant loss. We may remember the shock that we felt when we were told about the death of a friend or loved one. We may remember the anger over being told that we had lost our job. We may feel a sadness that reminds us of the end of a previous relationship. This kind of experience can be temporary. It may also remain for an extended period of time. A conversation with a friend or clergyperson can help us figure out if we need to do any further work in dealing with these earlier losses.

Grief is something we experience with a variety of intensities. Not everyone will respond in the same way about the closing of a church, for example. There are some people in the pews that may experience the closing of a church community as they would a death in the family. People may be upset, yet willing to move on to a new congregation. Some may actually be relieved of the burden of dealing with a dwindling congregation and a building that is consuming far too many resources.

A colleague was telling me of their experience in a rural congregation they were serving. They were holding a meeting to deal with some important business when it became clear that they could no longer function as a viable congregation. They interrupted their business and made the decision to close. There was a sense of relief that they could discuss this serious issue in a way in which they could arrive at some level of agreement. There would still be some sense of loss but the possibility of any complications could be minimized.

When a congregation closes we are ministering to a group of people who are going through their own personal experiences of grief. It is both impossible and unthinkable to recommend one way of dealing with this grief that will apply to everyone. Jeanette Auger writes, "each person experiences loss in their own unique way."[42] We are not just dealing with one person's grief. We are dealing with a group in which each person is at a different place in their journey. This will affect how we provide care and worship.

The intensity of grief may vary for any number of reasons. The intensity of grief may change as a person makes their way through the grief journey. In talking about the changing intensities of grief Colin Murray-Parkes writes, "Grief may be strong or weak, brief or prolonged, immediate or delayed; particular aspects of it may be distorted and symptoms that usually cause little trouble may become major sources of distress."[43]

Colin Murray-Parkes suggests that the level of attachment may affect how we grieve.[44] A person who is active in a given congregation may experience grief in a way that is completely different than a person who only occasionally attends Sunday morning service. A member of the choir or board, for example, may experience grief in a way that is different than someone involved in a midweek group. So much will depend on the time and energy a person offered the congregation. A lot will depend on the emotional attachment that develops around relationship, programming, worship and so on. When people develop strong attachments with a congregation it becomes increasingly difficult to let go and move on.

The intensity of a person's grief will also be affected by the "mode of death", "emergent life opportunities", and "level of stress". In other words, the way that a congregation has closed will be important in determining the intensity of someone's grief. There would seem to be a difference between a congregation making a decision for themselves and someone coming in from outside with the matter in hand. While there is a place for leadership within a denomination we need to be aware of the possible impact that this will have on a congregation's parishioners. A person's opportunities may help determine how their grief experience progresses.

What are the names and addresses of nearby congregations from within my chosen denomination? Are there any travel or property limitations I need to be aware of? What is going to happen with the church building and so on? A person's grief may be affected by the ultimate future of things like the building. Is the church building going to remain a place of worship or is it going to be converted into something like an academy for developing musicians? Is this going to be turned into a bar or a pool hall? Is there going to be enough time to complete our business or is this closure going to happen quickly?

We cannot complete a discussion on grief without dealing with the subject of time. After a recent funeral a member of the deceased's family was speaking with some of her friends. In talking about the service and the time leading up to it this family member made the curious comment that "At least it's all over now." What this person didn't seem to realize, however, was that the experience of grief does not end with the closing blessing of a funeral. It is not a question of turning off an emotional tap, so to speak. Grief is something that will be present with us for an extended period of time. Again, this will depend on the intensity of our connections and so on but it's important to remember that grieving is not something that can be rushed. We have become a society that has come to allow people a limited period of time in which to deal with grief. People will become impatient with friends who don't seem to be "getting over it". We may feel tempted to turn away from folks who constantly talk about what they have been through.

So how long will it take? While we cannot answer this definitively we can make some guesses and suggestions. Perhaps the most honest answer that we can offer is "A long time". There are some kinds of losses we will carry with us for the rest of our lives. There are other kinds of losses that will take considerably less time. There is a huge difference, for example, between losing a job and the death of a family member. Regardless of the time it takes we can share the optimism of a former patient of Dr. Oliver Sacks. When speaking to the eminent neurologist she said, "It is winter. I feel dead. But I know that spring will come again."[45]

In summarizing our comments on grief and loss we can quote Virginia Ironside when she writes, "Bereavement is a beastly business."[46] Ironside goes on to add, "This is the thing about bereavement—you can never tell how it will turn out, and any book or counselor that tells you otherwise is lying."[47] This is true for any living being. It can also be true for people living through the closure of their congregation. Dealing with any kind of loss is never easy. It certainly isn't something that we can take lightly.

Ministering to grieving people takes an almost infinite amount of time and patience. This kind of ministry takes a tremendous amount of energy. It is important, however, to take the necessary time and be a helpful presence for folks as they confront the kinds of losses that all too often enter our lives.

Chapter Four Checklist

- Grief is a natural response to many experiences in life. We all live through it at one time or another.
- Grief is also a normal response to the closure of our congregation.
- There can be many ways of experiencing and expressing our grief. There can be emotions and feelings we find confusing and frightening. We may intentionally or unintentionally target other people when dealing with these varied and intense emotions.
- There is no schedule for dealing with our grief. It's not something we can process in a set time period. Grieving takes time and energy.
- We can help grieving people by caring and listening. We can invite people to begin a journal and care for themselves in other ways. We can facilitate opportunities for people to talk and discuss their questions and feelings.
- We can acknowledge that grieving is difficult and help people move on to other tasks as the congregation moves towards closure.
- We can talk about our grief. We can also put our thoughts and feelings down on paper. We can begin a journal or simply write letters we can safely file away or run through a shredder.

Endnotes

1.   United Methodist Daily News, 20 January 1998
2.   Merkin, Dahne "Dreaming of Hitler: Passions and Provocations" (New York, 1997), pp. 91-92

3. Murray-Parkes, p.6
4. Ibid., P.9
5. Frye,   Northrop   "The   Educated   Imagination" (Bloomington, 1964), p.55
6. Riegel, Christian "Writing Grief: Margaret Lawrence and the Work of Mourning" (Winnipeg, 2003), p.9
7. Derrida, Jacques "The Work of Mourning" (Chicago and London, 2001), p.29
8. Pogue, Carolyn "Language of the Heart: Rituals, Stories and Information About Death" (Kelowna, 1998), p.55
9. Auger, p.191
10. Murray-Parkes, p.5
11. Auger, 2000, p.12
12. Heschel, p.366
13. Ending With Hope, p.58
14. Robertson introduces Michele Chaban (p. 175) as a person who has done some ground breaking work on Kubler-Ross's stages and outlines some of her work in this section as well.
15. Kuhl, p.xxiii
16. Ironside, Virginia "You'll Get Over It" (London, 1997), p.2
17. Robertson, p.80
18. Ibid, p.80
19. Ending With Hope, p.50
20. Murray-Parkes, p.43
21. Ibid, p.47
22. "Closed Church Still Beckons" Boston Globe, October 16th, 2003
23. Robertson, p.192
24. Murray-Parkes, p.80ff
25. Ending With Hope, p.59
26. Ironside, p.50
27. Ibid., p.60
28. Ending With Hope, p.46
29. Ironside, p.61-2

30. Ibid, P. 61-62
31. For a detailed discussion of battlefield exhaustion consult Terry Copp and Bill McAndrew's "Battle Exhaustion: Soldiers and Psychiatrists in the Canadian Army, 1939-45" (Kingston, 1990)
32 Kristeva, Julia. "Black Sun: Depression and Melancholia" (New York, 1987, 1989), p.34
33. Leas, P.45
34. Ibid, P.45
35. Morgan, John "Introduction" in "Loss and Grief" Edited by Neil Thompson (New York, 2002), p.ix
36. Jones, Ezra Earl "Strategies for New Churches" (New York, 1976), p.167
37. Auger, p.144
38. Ironside, p.31
39. Ibid., P.31
40. Quoted in Auger, p.189
41. Ibid, P.194
42. Ibid, p.67
43. Murray-Parkes, 1998, P.117
44. Ibid, P.119
45. Sacks, Oliver. "The Man Who Mistook His Wife For A Hat: And Other Clinical Tales." (New York, 1970, 1990), p.182
46. Ironside, p.x
47. Ibid, p.xvi

Chapter Five
Pastoral Care

In Ernest Hemmingway's timeless classic "The Old Man and the Sea" there is a touching scene in which the main character is fishing and hooks a female marlin. The marlin fought the fisherman until she tired and was landed in the boat. As this marlin was fighting for her life her male companion was swimming nearby. Hemmingway writes, "he stayed so close that the old man thought he would cut the line with his tail...." When the female marlin was finally in the boat her companion made one last leap from the water as if to confirm where the first marlin had finally landed. Hemmingway concludes the scene by observing, "He was beautiful, the old man remembered, and he stayed."[1]

"He stayed". These are powerful words that can help us see the importance of being present with people experiencing the closure of their congregation. This kind of commitment people have to one another permeates many aspects of life at sea. When a ship is in distress, for example, it is the responsibility of nearby ships to provide assistance. We can apply this same principle to congregations. Congregations within a given denomination have an opportunity to step in and offer some form of aid when a neighbour faces a challenge such as a closure. These responsibilities and possibilities will be outlined in this chapter as we consider the pastoral care people will need following the congregation's decision to close.

Bernard Moss has coined the term "imperative to care"2 and this can be applied when talking about the responsibilities of individuals and groups within a denomination for when a congregation decides to close. Two things that a closing congregation will need from a nearby congregation are people and support. The closure team can help coordinate this important work. In the Presbyterian Church (USA), for example, pastoral care is a priority for anyone working with a closing congregation.3 This should be the case in every denomination.

Paul has written about the "Body of Christ" and this is an important metaphor to include in our consideration here. The congregations within a given denomination gather to form a group or body. People share their gifts and skills with both their local congregations and the wider church. How do we care for the body of Christ when a congregation closes? How do we reach out and offer comfort and support when we are dealing with a group of people and not simply an individual?

One of the bonds that hold this body together is the relationship that so many people share with one another. Like ligaments around a wrist or an ankle, family and friends help work at bringing the community of faith together and keeping it strong. These folks need to be honored and cared for throughout the closing process. Relationships will be changed and in extreme cases they will end. As we have seen in the previous chapter on grief, this kind of change and loss will have an effect on people.

How can we help people find their way through these changes? How can we help people deal with the loneliness that can result from changing relationships? People may be saying "Goodbye" to friends who have been an important part of their lives. These folks have contributed to one another's lives for years. They have shared in the times of joy and celebration. They have welcomed people through baptism and raised a glass at weddings. They have also shared in times of loss and grief, having wept at all too many funerals. They have said "Goodbye" to people who have moved to another community. There may be gaps that appear in people's lives. There may be spaces and silences that can be difficult to deal with.

Relationships within the church tend to become increasingly important, as we grow older. As friends move or pass away isolation may creep in to people's lives and this isolation can have significant effects on our quality of life. As we grow older and our health changes, traveling may become more difficult as well. One of the things that happen when we reach a certain point in life is that we are no longer able to drive a vehicle. If our church closes we may not be able to attend another within the same denomination. This affects our social circle and the availability of people to provide assistance and companionship. This may lead to a tendency to "disengage" from the world around us.[4] Eminent psychiatrist C.G. Jung wrote, "… no living creature adjusts itself easily and smoothly to new conditions."[5]

The church can provide a place where people can remain committed and connected in a way in which their social and spiritual needs can be met. These connections can help us confront this temptation to "disengage" and pull away from the people around us. Closing a person's congregation may affect their lives in ways that are more profound than we may anticipate. It is important to consider these factors in how we offer pastoral care and support. These factors can be spiritual, psychological and practical. We care for people when we listen. We also care for people when we help them find transportation to their new congregations.

Before we move too far into this discussion it is important

to clarify some issues around what we are trying to accomplish when we are offering pastoral care to the people in a closing congregation. Clarifying some of the terminology frequently used in palliative care circles is important. This helps us respond to some of the situations in which parishioners find themselves.

One of the words that may be used a lot is "healing". However, we have to be careful whenever we use this word. Heather Robertson writes, "Healing is another of those ambiguous, overworked words that mean all things to all people."[6] For me, healing is a concept fundamentally different than cure. "Cure" is another word we may not always understand. We cure an ailment of some sort. We help the body restore itself following an illness or injury. A cure is simply physical whereas healing is something that can affect us spiritually and psychologically. Healing is something that can rebuild and renew relationships in a way that brings a peace that helps us move on with life. Closing a congregation, for example, can place a lot of strain on friendships. The effort to bring healing can deal with the important issues and challenges dividing people at a critical time in life. This kind of healing is important for when a congregation closes.

The wider church can share in this pastoral care by offering any available expertise that can be provided by a staff person or volunteer. Many congregations are developing visitation teams of trained lay people who may be useful when a congregation closes. When it comes to caring for the people of a closing congregation many of the principles that we will be discussing have been borrowed from disciplines such as palliative care. Palliative care is something that normally applies to individuals facing life-threatening conditions. Figuring out how to apply these principles to a group of people will be a challenge. What does palliative care look like for a congregation? We can also ask a few related questions. These questions are important as we try to respond to the congregation's pastoral care needs. How do we make a group of very different people comfortable? How can we control the collective and individual pain that may be experienced? How can we help people make the closing of a church as smooth and painless as possible? Heather Robertson writes, "The philosophy of hospice and palliative care is to enhance the quality of life remaining to us, not to shorten or lengthen it."[7]

Dame Cicely Saunders offers her own thoughts on this kind of approach when she writes, "The essence of hospice care is the giving of a secure continuity of support that frees the patient and family to turn to their own priorities."[8] Saunders goes on to suggest, "hospice care is not restricted to buildings but comprises attitudes and skills that can be deployed anywhere."[9] Hospice care focuses on people. It focuses on the individual patient and the people who share their lives.

All of this is important when working with a closing congregation. In helping a congregation close we are not helping it survive for any extended period of time. We are not trying to feed any hopes of a rescue that will never take place. We are trying to help a group of people complete any business related to the closure. We are trying to help maintain the quality of life for a closing congregation while it attempts to build a legacy.

An important part of this work is helping a congregation with the pain a closure causes. As we have just identified, dealing with a person's pain is one of the central features of palliative care. Jeanette Auger suggests that palliative care "means to lessen pain without hope of cure."[10]

Pain can be experienced in different ways.[11] It can be physical, spiritual or psychological. How do we respond to these kinds of pain, as they may be a part of a person's response to a closing congregation? There may be something we can do.

In discussing the pain a congregation may experience, we can name the two rules of pain management outlined by

David Kuhl. These two rules are: "Pain is what (the patient) says it is and not what I or others think it ought to be; and second, the right dose of pain medication for (the patient) is the dose that eliminates the pain."[12] People would tell me how they were doing with the closure of my previous congregation. They would describe experiences and encounters. Some of these folks were also telling me how they were feeling. They were trying to describe their emotional responses to what was happening. In listening to what they had to say it would have been inappropriate for me to tell them that their experience was somehow "right" or "wrong". They were sharing what reality looked like for them and it was important to respect that. I may have agreed or disagreed with them but it was not my place to share those thoughts. I couldn't say to someone, for example, "Come on, isn't that an overreaction?" We cannot tell people how they should be responding to the things that are happening in their lives. We can only listen and try to understand where they are "coming from". We can be a helpful presence while they try and figure things out for themselves.

In caring for people David Kuhl suggests three words that are important. These three words are: "truth", "touch" and "time".[13] These are three important words that will figure prominently in the care and attention we offer. They will help us understand the many different ways in which we can respond to people's loss and grief. They can help us respond when people come to us in search of a listening ear or a helping hand.

The first word Kuhl mentions is "truth". We hear this word so often it becomes almost impossible to define it. We can understand Pilate's confusion when he hears the term and wonders, "What is truth?" When we tell the truth we deal with the situation as it really is. We can talk about what is really going on in the congregation. We can talk about our true thoughts and feelings. People do not like having their time and energy wasted. One of the ways in which we can increase the level of openness and honesty is by creating the appropriate atmosphere for people to find out what is happening. We can provide an inviting space for people to share their thoughts and questions. We can offer an inviting place for people to share in their opinions and discussion. We can also ensure that the information they receive is an accurate reflection of what is really going on.

One of the ways in which we can help people deal with the loss and loneliness that can be experienced in congregational closures is to encourage friends to "stay in touch". Touching is both important to our physical and psychological health.[14] Kuhl writes, "'Touch' means to have contact with another person, it means there is a connection between people. Suffering is reduced and pain altered."[15] Kuhl adds, "Physical contact—that is, touch—is an essential ingredient to a sense of emotional connectedness."[16] We can hug a person or simply hold their hand. It would be best to let them name the boundaries and identify what they need, however. Touching can be misunderstood. Not everybody likes being hugged and we have to respect that. People can often offer clues as to how we can respond.

The work of telling the truth and reaching out takes time. Humans are not always effective communicators so it may take some time to get our thoughts and feelings organized. It may take us a while to put our thoughts and feelings into words so that we can express them in a way that others can understand. It may take even more effort to hear people and figure out what they are trying to tell us. There are times when human communication is like watching two people speak in completely different languages. Information cannot get through until someone is able to break the code and move the conversation along.

Perhaps the one thing that helps us persist when we are trying to reach out in these kinds of situations is to trust others. In their book entitled "Leadership", Warren Bennis and Burt Nanus claim that trust is the one thing that can hold an organization together.[17] They also go on to comment on how difficult the concept of trust can be to understand. It's not something we can easily define. In a number of ways it is like glue. It holds things together even though we may have no idea of how it works. What we can say here is that trust can include things like "accountability, predictability and reliability".[18] This can also be important to relationships as well as organizations and congregations.

Trust is an important ingredient here as it helps free people to speak and listen in a way that improves the chances for the grace and health that has been mentioned earlier. Simply put, trust is the belief that someone is being open and honest with us. It's a hope and an expectation that we will be valued, respected and treated fairly. David Kuhl writes, "The truth teller must be able to trust that the listener will not judge but will simply seek to understand."[19] This trust helps build an atmosphere of safety so that people can access and come to grips with the past. They can struggle with the things they have done and also the things they have not done. Jennie Wilting writes, "Knowing where and whom to trust is one of the most important essentials for good human relationships."[20] Any uncertainty may increase the amount of stress experienced by individuals and the people around them.

We have already discussed the effects that bereavement can have on a person's health. What we will deal with here is the toll that stress and conflict can take on a person. Appropriate amounts of stress can help keep us moving through life at a healthy pace. It is normal, for example, to be stressed out before a preaching assignment or any other public speaking commitment. The state of being "nervous" can free up energy to help us through our challenge. I begin to worry when I don't feel the "butterflies" before a sermon. I begin to wonder if there is something wrong. There are healthy levels of stress that help us through life.

Excessive amounts of stress, however, can build up and

negatively affect us in the long run. Jennie Wilting writes that stress "is a factor that induces bodily and mental tension."[21] Wilting adds, "Stress occurs whenever the body is faced with a threat to its integrity and then the body goes into a state of alarm." This is only the beginning of a process that can leave us drained and burned out. Certain physical reactions help us deal with any situation we interpret to be a threat of some sort. These natural reactions give us the energy needed to deal with this supposed threat. They are only intended to be temporary reactions, however.

I was at a meeting at the local town hall one evening when a committee member's fire department pager went off. When she heard that there was a house fire she was out of the meeting room in a hurry. People quickly left the meeting to go home and take care of children while spouses responded to the alarm. Meanwhile, I stood on the steps of the town hall and watched the activity at the fire hall next door. Within moments vehicles appeared from almost out of nowhere. They came to a screeching halt near the fire hall and people jumped out. As I was watching the response a voice called out from behind me, "Watch out!" Just as I moved out of the way two guys ran by still wearing their hockey uniforms. I was told later that one of the players hadn't even realized that he was still wearing his ice skates. These volunteers were experiencing an adrenaline rush that helped them respond to the fire and get the job done. They couldn't sustain this rush for very long, however. Physical exhaustion would soon set in and their effectiveness would begin to fade.

I remember a conversation over coffee with a friend while the situation in my previous congregation was reaching a crisis point. He was describing some dental work he was having later that day. I told him how sorry I was that he needed to go through this when he waved my comments off saying, "This will be over in a couple of hours. What you're experiencing will continue long after I've left the dentist's office." This certainly offered a new perspective on the situation. His comments certainly cast a light onto the difference between the normal stresses as all face every day as opposed to that which affects us in the long term.

Stress affects us physically and emotionally, and it takes its toll when it continues for an extended period of time. People need to keep an eye on their own well-being. One of the realities in any long-term situation in which people are under a lot of stress is the potential for something called "Post Traumatic Stress Disorder", or PTSD. Things that are happening to us, and around us, can build up to a point where our system is threatened with collapse. We don't always know that it is happening until something happens that wakes us up to reality. This build-up can lead to burn out, collapse, or worse. There may be a morning when we cannot find the energy to climb out of bed. There may be an incident or confrontation at work that is beyond our normal everyday behavior.

When we talk about dealing with stress, and caring for one another we can also encourage leaders to look after themselves. This kind of "self-care" is important and very personal. We have to look after ourselves and that includes being aware of our personal thoughts, feelings and overall health. There are many resources that can help us develop a healthy way of managing our lives and caring for ourselves. I'll briefly mention a couple of important things here. In looking to improve our lives, we have to be observing routine things such as watching what we eat and finding more time to exercise. Walking, for example, is a simple way of dealing with stress. There may be other relaxation techniques that we may find helpful. My spouse has developed an interest in yoga and talks about how this has helped her deal with stress in her workplace. The main thing is to keep looking until we find something that works for us. We can ask our friends and colleagues what they do. We can pay attention to the media. We can find something that interests us and turn this into a hobby. Many people find gardening, and even housework, to be cathartic or relaxing. There are many different possibilities.

In dealing with stress we should also set aside time for reading, prayer and writing. We cannot forget the social aspect of our lives either. It seems all too easy to forget our family and friends when we face a time of enduring stress and conflict. Finding time for the people in our lives is an important way of looking after ourselves. This may sound trite or obvious but when things get tough, and the schedule fills up, self-care can be one of the first things to go out the window. The phone begins ringing and people call out for our energy and attention. The situation may build to crisis point where we may begin wondering if we can hold on until the closing process is complete. Our emotional gas tank, so to speak, may run out and we will be left high and dry. Looking after ourselves and building a strong support network is an important way of dealing with any crisis in life. We cannot offer this kind of reminder often enough.

In caring for ourselves, Wilting writes, "The goal in dealing with stress is not to avoid stress altogether but to use stress in a positive rather than in a negative way…"[22] Wilting adds, "We have more control over our lives and circumstances than we often realize."[23] The priority here is to find out how we can control what is happening in our lives. One of the things we can do is examine our expectations of others and ourselves. What are our priorities and commitments? What standards have we established for ourselves?

When I graduated from seminary I held colleagues, in particular, to a high standard. It reached a point where one of my local colleagues sat me down over coffee and observed that I was expecting far too much of the people around me. It becomes all too easy to resent or carry a grudge when the people around us fail to live up to some standard we set for them. We have to be realistic in dealing with the people and situations around us. One of the values of St. Christopher's Hospice is their assertion that no one is perfect.[24] This may seem overly simplistic but it is difficult to keep in mind when we are working with human beings. It is important that we become effective in whatever work we take on. There is a difference, however, between effectiveness and perfection. It is important that we continue learning and practicing our skills. We have to keep learning from our mistakes.

There are several ways in which people experience stress when a congregation closes. We may experience stress when someone acts disagreeably. We experience stress when an event unfolds in an unplanned manner. How many times have we seen hopes and dreams change as we try and live them out? We need to find a way of dealing with things as they happen. We have to find a way of coping with all of the surprises that come our way. A European general once said, "no plan survives an encounter with the enemy." I've heard of athletes making similar observations when it comes to their respective sports. None of our plans will work out perfectly. We have to be ready to make changes when they are necessary.

This reality is true in all of our lives. A number of years ago I watched a movie in which the main character used the words "improvise, adapt, and overcome". These three words offer a simple formula for dealing with the changes that can all too suddenly appear our lives. I have come to use these words a great deal in the congregations I have served. I have used these words so often that friends of mine made a sign out of them. This sign was placed on a wall in their office for everyone to see. I think that this is a testimony to how these words can help us deal with all of the things that happen in life. There are times when things don't go according to plan and we have to "improvise, adapt and overcome".

When things in my previous congregation began spinning out of control the stress was really taking its toll. I was tired and cranky. I wasn't sleeping well at all. There were times when even routine decisions were increasingly difficult. These are some of the signs to watch for so that we know its time to take a break and do something different for a while. Ian Black describes a similar experience that he shares on his website "Calling Time", "Holding the frustration and impatience, together with the unresolved pain of those campaigning to save 'their church' during this time took far more out of me than I imagined and it was not very pleasant".[25] I find myself telling people that we are no good to the congregation if we are burned out wrecks. Congregations need leaders who can function effectively and self-care, as we have previously discussed, is an important part of this effectiveness.

When we care for ourselves we model something that others can see and use. We show them a healthy example of someone coping with a difficult situation. Jennie Wilting writes, "One of the best ways to teach others to behave in healthy ways is to be a role model of healthy behavior.... Others tend to learn more from how you behave than from what you say."[26] Wilting adds, "In dealing with ourselves and others in problematic situations, we need to take responsibility for our own behavior, feelings and ideas rather than blaming or excusing others or blaming or excusing ourselves."[27] Our response to any given situation can be an example for others to see and apply to their own lives.[28]

I remember a dinner conversation with a person who was finding retirement difficult. He had invested so much of his time and energy into his professional life but had no idea what he was going to do once the job was complete and it was time to move on. When my spouse and I were on our way home from this dinner she looked at me and said, "You'd better think seriously about getting a hobby before you retire!" This has been advice people have been offering throughout my years of ministry. We can get so caught up in what we are doing in the congregation we lose touch with who we are away from the office. Hobbies distract us and give us a mental break. We can focus and use our energies in a different way. Many people will start a garden while others will work on restoring antique cars. Exercise is another way to unwind and get out of the office. It's important that we find activities away from the congregation so that we can refocus and renew our energies for the work of serving parishioners.

One of these activities can be keeping a journal. In the chapter on grief we discussed the possibility of writing as a way of dealing with our thoughts and feelings about the loss we experience. We can talk about the importance of writing here as well. As we have mentioned before, journals offer the opportunity to write things down and relieve some of the pressure that builds during stressful situations. We can also write down our thoughts and impressions. We can share our thinking on what we see as the options and possibilities for a situation.

There are times when we can find the necessary decision making easier once we see something put in writing. Keeping a journal will also provide a helpful resource for later use. We can use the journal to review our experience of a situation for decision-making purposes. We can also use the journal as a source for creating the necessary documentation in the event of more formal proceedings at the conclusion of the closure process. When we move into our chapter on conflict we will further discuss the possibilities around appeals, official complaints and so on. Journals are a helpful tool in helping us respond to these situations. Time and emotions can affect our memories to a point in which it might affect the steps taken after the actual closing of the congregation. Journals help us remember and they help us find a calm and centered space so that we can deal with the chaos around us.

One clergyperson described the journey that her congregation made towards closure as one that was "graceful and healthy".[29] We can all hope for this kind of grace and health but it doesn't always work out this way, regardless of the coping mechanisms we may try. As we have been discussing throughout this book, things don't always go according to plan. There have been closures that are neither "graceful" nor "healthy". When we consider the challenges of any closure we can be reminded that listening is an important skill, especially for those who lead worship throughout the time in which a congregation is closing.[30]

One of the things that we can keep in mind is that the time leading up to the closing of a congregation can be seen as an opportunity for people to unload what is in their minds and hearts. We can let them say what they want. David Kuhl writes, "I had to respect that whatever those people were saying was their own truth, their reality..."[31] We have to listen with both our ears and our hearts. This is an important way of showing both compassion and empathy. One of the ways in which we can do this is by creating a place where people feel accepted and by including as many parishioners as possible in any discussion involving the closure of the congregation.[32] People can thus have a chance to tell their story as well as hear what others have to say. The closure team can facilitate this kind of conversation. The entire team can participate or name an individual team member to be present for these kinds of conversations.

One possibility for providing an opportunity for people to share what is in their minds and hearts is the offering of an evening where people can tell of their experiences in their congregation. It's an idea that I have heard from a number of sources. They can talk about the good times they have experienced. They can also talk about the challenging times and problems needing to be dealt with. While a tremendous amount of care needs to be shown in leading these kinds of events they may be a helpful way of offering people the opportunity of telling their story. It may also be a way of improving the level of communication within the congregation.

Effective communication is an important way of caring for one another. It's not something that we are good at necessarily. I remember talking with a colleague who wanted a nickel for every time someone named "communication" as a challenge in his or her marriage. This is ironic, considering the central place communication has in how we relate to one another as human beings. Talking is important, but it is not the entire story. Listening is important as well as the attention we pay to the content of the message in which we are trying to send.

I often find myself wrestling with whether or not I am an effective listener. Not everyone has what it takes to be completely present with someone who needs to talk. Effective listening takes time, patience, and openness. We don't always have to agree with what a person says but we have to make the attempt to understand what they may be trying to tell us. In discussing the development of critical listening skills Heather Robertson writes, "Attentive listening requires sensitivity to nuance, emotion, facial expression, and body language. Listen. Shut up and listen."[33]

Part of this listening will happen when we work at finding out more about the congregation. People may want to talk about the past. They may want to talk about what has happened in the congregation through the years. They may want to name the good times and the troubles. They may even want to release some of the secrets or release the skeletons in the closet that have been haunting the congregations. They may want to release the burden of the past so that they can move on with "a clean slate" so to speak.

Sometimes we underestimate the importance of the past. One of my interests is Canadian history. I remember a recent article on the Canadian province of Newfoundland and Labrador where the writer states, "...history is an unbroken tale of mistakes and missed opportunities."[34] Any national, local, and congregational history could be described this way. Each of our congregations can look into their pasts and see an "unbroken tale of mistakes and missed opportunities." What has happened to make the congregation the way it is today? What didn't happen? The key is to examine the 'mistakes" and "missed opportunities". We can learn from them and attempt to reduce the chances of history repeating itself. We can also see what else has happened. What have been the highlights in a particular congregation? Was there a building project that had been successfully completed? Was there an outreach project that met a need in the community? These stories need to be told as a way of giving importance and meaning to the presence and life of a congregation. It's also a way of offering learnings and inspiration for people as they move on to their new congregations where they can perhaps make valuable contributions.

One of the ways in which we can delve into the history of our congregation is by doing something called a "life review". David Kuhl describes a life review as "looking in the rearview mirror" as we travel.[35] Kuhl writes, "It seems that a life story, or life review includes a component of grief. It also contains love, joy, gratitude, pride, laughter and hope. For some, it includes guilt and shame..." Examining the past will relieve us of the burdens that can weigh us down.

Examining the past can also help in some of the "anticipatory preparation"[36] that will happen as we make our way towards the actual closing of the congregation's doors. When we anticipate something we can build a picture of what the future will hold. We can research information about a congregation we will be visiting. We can find out more about the kind of ministry they offer. This will be a source of hope and support as we make our way through the different aspects of the closure process. Our efforts to care for parishioners can include the introduction to new possibilities.[37] A life review for a congregation can help with much of this "anticipatory preparation". We can see where the congregation has been. We can figure out what we want and where we are going.

How do we actually look back and review our lives? What does a life review look like? How can we build one within the context of our congregations? Perhaps the best way of doing a life review is by picturing a tree.[38] It is something we can include in a diagram for everyone to see. We can draw it on a large piece of newsprint or create a slide using the latest computer technology. Our first step would be to look at the places in our lives where there would be major "branching points". What were the main events in our lives? Was it a marriage or an accomplishment of some sort? Was it a job or move that turned out well? What were the important experiences and encounters?

For me, one of these "branching out" moments was my move from Canada's east coast to the western province of Alberta. I was both nervous and terrified, as I had never done anything like this before. People in the congregation can be offered a chance to identify their own "branching out" moments. As we have already mentioned, parishioners may look at programs and projects that reached out and helped people in the neighbouring community. We may consider the ministry of a particular person or the leadership of a group. We can look at what the congregation has contributed to the wider body of Christ. These may be some of the important "branching" moments that help a congregation find its place. In discussing the beginning point in a life review David Kuhl writes, "Life review begins with remembering and reflecting on the past, the choices you've made, your sense of self, your relationship with others, and your connection to a higher power such as God."[39]

A second step in a life review is traveling down some of these branches and the examination of the family of origin.[40] How was the congregation created? Did an individual or group from a nearby congregation of the same denomination plant it? Did a group from a neighbourhood come together and build the congregation from the ground up? In one congregation's case a neighbourhood family began holding meetings in their own home and people from their community came for meetings, Bible studies and so on. This group contributed to a point where they found a piece of land and continued growing the congregation. A life review can track the growth of this congregation from the time of its creation to the present moment.

The next step can examine this development and identify the time when the church was at its peak. People will talk about the times when their congregations had a strong attendance, and a Sunday school numbering in the hundreds or even thousands. They will remember a time when the finances were sound and they were having a hard time keeping up with all the changes. We can call this time the "Golden Age" of the congregation. There may be some question as to whether or not these "Golden Years" really existed but that is beside the point. Our priority is listening to people as they talk about their experiences with a congregation.

In naming a "Golden Age" for the congregation we can also find and name the low point in the life of the congregation. Was there a time when the congregation struggled to remain open? Was there a challenge that people had to work in overcoming? How did the congregation recover? The kind of hard work that goes in to these kinds of recoveries can be something people can be thankful for.

One thing to be careful of in any life review is the kind of emotional baggage such a process can bring out. People may get depressed and angry at what they discover. We may experience emotions like anger and rage. We may be shocked and surprised at what our clergy and friends have said and done. We may be surprised at how we respond to some of the things that come to our attention. A life review can surprise us in ways that are both life giving and troubling. We have to tread carefully when digging around in the past.

One of the reasons for treading carefully is that we all have secrets. David Kuhl writes, "Individuals, families, groups, and organizations keep secrets. In turn, secrets keep individuals, secrets keep families, secrets isolate and hold their keepers hostage. Essentially, people keep secrets and secrets keep people."[41] Secrets are tough on us as they limit how we can respond to a situation. Secrets prevent clarity and intimacy that is important in any relationship. Secrets come in different shapes and sizes. Former board members may have made serious mistakes with the financial resources of the congregation. It's important for people to be open to the secrets that emerge from any effort to review the life of the congregation. David Kuhl writes, "We share a deep sense of relief that the unspeakable had finally been spoken."[42] We have to speak the unspeakable, to use Kuhl's words.

Another reason why dealing with history is so important is because it is a central piece of who we are. Our history is an important part of our identity. Many things go into the mix of who we are. I am both an ordained minister and a spouse. I am a Canadian male who was born and raised in the province of New Brunswick. For many of us, our faith is an important part of who we are. This may extend to the congregation to which we have committed ourselves. When these congregations close there may be implications for our personal identities.[43] In thinking about changes to our identities Murray-Parkes writes, "...it takes time for individuals to realize and accept the change in themselves which follows a majour loss."[44] This could affect how we see ourselves and how we relate to the people around us.

There are many ways of relating to people and caring for them. In his book entitled "Resurrection" Leo Tolstoy offers a list of laws coming out of the Sermon on the Mount.[45] There are two of these "laws" that can help us find a way to care for people whose congregation is closing. The first law is based on Matthew 5: 38-42 and concerns Jesus' advice to "turn the other cheek". This is a difficult, and frequently frustrating piece of scripture. It is something we can all work towards, however, in an emotionally charged process like the closing of a church. People will be angry about what is going on, and they will be tempted to "lash out". We have to find a way of dealing with both our own anger and our response to the anger of others.

A second "law" that will be helpful is related to the first, and can be found in Matthew 5: 43-44. This is the section of the Sermon on the Mount where Jesus tells his followers to love their enemies. This helps us relate to the people with whom we will be working. When emotions are running high, we may experience the all too human temptation to run and hide. We may also experience the temptation to label someone negatively and dismiss what they have to say without giving it much consideration. While self-preservation is a natural instinct, it may not be all that helpful when dealing with a hurting group of people. We may not always like whom we are dealing with but it is helpful in the long run to do what we can to manage the situation. Both of these "laws" will be helpful when we deal with conflict in our next chapter. They will be helpful when we consider the disagreements we encounter and the hard work it takes to make our way through these disagreements.

One of the challenges facing the closure team is the assessment of cultural differences within and between congregations. This is based on what Jeanette Auger suggests, when she writes, "It is crucial that the health care provider becomes aware of the cultural needs of the patients."[46] There are differences in how people of different cultures respond to loss and grief. It's important we become acquainted with these differences as they may apply to what is happening in a congregation. Auger offers the example that "In the east the articulation of love and caring is mute, in the west it is vocal."[47] This kind of information gathering is important when the closure team is working with a congregation serving First Nations people, for example.

The biblical image that can help us understand the changes that are happening is that of the people making their way into the wilderness. William Bridges calls this time the "Neutral Zone".[48] This refers to the time when people leave the comfort of the familiar in uncertainty of an unknown, and perhaps even hostile place. We no longer have the routines and relationships that have been a consistent part of our lives. We may feel disoriented as we find our way towards the new beginnings that lie ahead. We may feel the temptation to resist this journey, as we do not always like silence and emptiness. How many people need to have the radio on as they do their chores around the house or drive around in their cars? How many have purchased some sort of so-called "white noise machines" that provide enough background sounds to help them sleep? What happens when the music stops?

Bridges compares this wilderness time with crossing the street.[49] Once we get started we have to keep going if we are to reduce the chance of injury or worse. How many times did the people of Israel want to return to Egypt? How many times did Moses have to keep them moving?

Another way of looking at this time in the wilderness is to compare it with the "time-out" that is called in many sports like football. A time-out can stop the clock so that the coach and players can plan the next play and make any changes in strategy that can help improve their chances of winning. We evaluate the game and plan for what is going to happen. It can also be a time to rest before the next play. This in-between time can be as important as the actual game itself. Decisions made in the wilderness can be as important as any made within the context of the congregation.

One of the most important opportunities in the wilderness is the time to be alone. Like a time-out in a football or basketball game we have the opportunity to think about what is ahead and plan our next move. We can remember and find out what has been meaningful for us in the previous congregation. We can decide on what will be important in our next congregation. What did we like in the previous congregation? What will we be looking for in the next place? Another question that we can ask is one that is common to interviews with clergy and students experiencing the call to ministry. This question deals with our hopes and dreams for a congregation uniquely suited to our personal gifts and abilities. What is our ideal congregation? It's kind of like naming the things that would go into a dream house. We may not get what we want but we may get some insight into which we are and what we are looking for in life. It may be helpful to deal with these questions by creating a series of written lists. Once we see this material in writing we may develop a better sense of where we are going and what we will be doing.

When we find ourselves in a wilderness place it can be tempting to turn around and try to leave. We may also find ourselves tempted to race through it. We have to resist the temptation and take our time to think things through. When we are in the forest and don't take our time to find out where we are then we risk running around in circles or getting lost. We may be running fast but we really aren't going anywhere. In fact, we may wind up in worse shape then when we entered the wilderness in the first place. We have to take our time so that we can find our bearings. We have to make sure we don't miss anything important. When we run through the forest we can miss both the beauty of what is around us and we can also miss the danger signals. We may miss the paw print, or steaming pile of animal waste that tells us we are not alone. Taking our time can mean any number of things. It could mean paying a second visit to a congregation we have been to the previous Sunday. It could mean the scheduling a coffee appointment with the minister so that some questions can be asked and information shared. We want to be sure that when we come out of the wilderness we can find the Promised Land in which we can live and renew our journeys.

One of the things that we may face in the wilderness is our fear. Fear is something we have talked about earlier and we can consider it here as well. When we experience the wilderness we confront the unknown. When we confront the unknown we may respond by experiencing fear. Speed Leas writes, "Fear is what you experience emotionally when you perceived that you are being threatened by danger or evil and you feel incompetent to manage it."[50] A lot of conflict comes out of the experience of fear. If we can somehow find a way of dealing with these fears the potential for conflict is, again, reduced.

There are many ways of dealing with fear. If someone is afraid of the dark we can turn on a light. We show them that there is nothing to worry about. When fear comes out of a lack of knowledge we can work at educating people. We can help people find sources of information that can help give them a more accurate picture of what is going on. What other kinds of fear can be experienced when a church closes? One of the main fears is that of rejection. There may be uncertainty as to how people will respond when we commit to a new congregation. We may be worried about whether or not people will like us. We may be worried about whether or not people will accept and include us. We may be afraid of the unknown. What will things be like when the doors close and we move on?

In discussing the possible responses to fear Leas writes, "Nothing works better in dealing with fear than direct, calm assurance on the part of the leader that the idea of disaster you are now anticipating is not likely to come to fruition."[51] We have to be calm and this can include anything from our body language to our tone of voice. We have to be clear when describing what is going on. We have to be careful about what we say. We may think that an off the cuff comment is harmless and be surprised at the results of what we say. This includes the respecting of any confidences we have been asked to keep.

Fear is one of the things that keep us from letting go and moving on. "Letting go" is important. David Kuhl shares a Hindu story about hunters developing a proven way to trap monkeys. Kuhl writes, "A half coconut would be hollowed out, and a hole made that was only large enough to let the a monkey's open hand pass through. The coconut was then pinned to the ground and tempting food placed beneath the coconut. A monkey would approach, intent on getting hold of the food beneath the coconut, but as soon as it grasped the food in its fist, it found itself unable to pull its hand and food free from the coconut. Imprisoned it would stay, caught by its own unwillingness to open its fist."[52]

Letting go has been an important spiritual practice for centuries. A number of people have intentionally left the cares and concerns of the world behind and find their way to remote locations where they can focus their time and energy on spiritual matters. The Christian tradition has had its many communities of monks and individual hermits. Hindus have their "renouncers". There have also been similar people in the Buddhist tradition. These "renouncers" are people who turn their backs on the world to find a higher state of being.[53]

We can apply a similar kind of discipline in our effort to let go of things like church buildings and committee work. Moving on becomes difficult when we keep our fists around things like bricks and mortar. Moving on becomes difficult when we try and hang on to the past. Each of us will be letting go in different ways. People who have been used to working hard in keeping a congregation open will be finding a different way of relating to a congregation. There may be a change in that they will be receiving instead of giving.[54] This can be a major shift in how someone sees and understands their world.

As we discuss all of the different ways in which we can care for the people of our closing congregations we can keep one principal in mind. We can be reminded of the words contained in the physician's Hippocratic oath. A commitment is made to "first, do no harm". People can experience pain and suffering simply by having painful encounters with the professionals who help them. David Kuhl suggests that these kinds of negative encounters are far more common than we would think.[55] We minimize pain and suffering when we listen. We help the situation by trying to understand and communicate. We reduce the anxiety level by showing humanity and compassion. When we try to think of something in response to a parishioner's question we can make it a priority to "do no harm". This will affect how we choose our words. It will affect how we respond. These are important words to hold in our minds and hearts when caring for the people around us.

Chapter Five Checklist

- Closing a congregation is difficult work for the individuals involved. What kind of spiritual and psychological assistance will be needed to help them with this work?
- Who will be providing pastoral care for the congregation? What will they need to do in order to provide this care?
- What will be the denominational involvement in providing this pastoral care?
- Are there any program staff people available to provide educational and healing opportunities for parishioners and members of the closure team?
- Who will provide pastoral care for the clergy leaders and other staff people?
- Is there any financing available to help fund any kind of professional assistance?
- Take a lesson from one of the most important parts of the physician's Hippocratic Oath: Do no harm.

Endnotes

1. Hemmingway, Ernest "The Old Man and the Sea" (New York, 1952, 1980), P. 49-50
2. Thompson, p.39
3. Presbyterian Church USA web page—Constitutional Musings: Note 1
4. Whalley, p.37
5. Storr, Anthony "The Essential Jung: Selected Writings" (Princeton, 1983), p.52
6. Robertson, p.83
7. Ibid., p.76

8. Thompson, p .23
9. Ibid, p.23
10. Auger, p.74
11. Kuhl, p.xvii
12. Ibid., p.77
13. Ibid., p.64
14. Ibid., p.105
15. Ibid., p.99
16. Ibid., p.113
17. Bennis, Warren and Nanus, Bert "Leadership" (New York, 1997), p.41
18. Ibid., p.41
19. Kuhl, p.176
20. Wilting, p.130
21. Wilting, p.81
22. Ibid., p.81
23. Ibid., p.82
24. Thompson, p.24-25
25. Black, Ian "Calling Time" (Personal Website)
26. Wilting, p.xi
27. Ibid, p.xiii
28. Ibid, p.29
29. Ending With Hope, P.43
30. Ramshaw, Elaine "Ritual and Pastoral Care" (Minneapolis, 1987), P.18
31. Kuhl, p.xxi
32. Ending With Hope, p.52
33. Robertson, p.111
34. Bannister, Jerry "Whigs and Nationalists: The Legacy of Judge Prowse's 'The History of Newfoundland'" in Acadiensis, Autumn 2002, p.99
35. Kuhl, 2002, p.140
36. Murray-Parkes, 1998, p.209
37. Ibid., p.209)
38. David Kuhl suggests this process and bases his work on that of Birren and Duetchman, 2002, p.141

39. Kuhl, p.156
40. Ibid., p.142
41. Ibid., p.172
42. Ibid., p.xvii
43. Ibid., p.94
44. Ibid., p.99
45. Tolstoy, Leo "Resurrection" (New York, 1999Ed.), p.482
46. Auger, p.139
47. Ibid., p.142ff
48. Bridges, p.112
49. Ibid., p.112
50. Leas, p.49
51. Ibid., p.61
52. Kuhl, p.259-260
53. Flood, Gavin "An Introduction to Hinduism" (Cambridge, 1996, 1999), P.13ff
54. Thompson, p.24
55. Kuhl, p.61

Chapter Six
Conflict

It has happened in all too many cities with professional sports teams. Early one morning people open the morning newspaper to find out their beloved team is moving to another city. The team is being promised such goodies as a new stadium and profits beyond belief. The ownership group holds a press conference and their spokespeople spin a series of empty clichés before leaving town in their private jets. When this news sinks in there is usually an organized response in which fans get together in an effort to save their team. There are signs and protests but precious little is accomplished. The decision has been made and fans seem powerless to stop the process. This "Save the Team" movement receives a lot of media attention but, as expected, the team leaves anyway.

It may seem strange to see this situation outlined as an introduction for a chapter on conflict. One thing that emerges when a team leaves a community is the difference that develops between the team's fan base and ownership. Their values and worldviews are different. The way they understand the business, and how decisions are made, may be different as well. These differences often lead to public disagreements and protests. People may try to take advantage of every opportunity to get their point across to a higher authority and a wider audience.

A congregation in trouble can find itself in the same situation. Conflict can emerge as a reality for the people facing the task of closing their congregation. Gary McIntosh writes, "Students of physics tell us that any movement will produce friction."[1] Any effort to gather a group of individuals to accomplish a given task can have this same effect. Their differences may work to help accomplish a collective task but there will still be disagreement and friction.

A couple of years ago a pair of visitors came to church one Sunday morning. They claimed to be representing a group from the surrounding community and were offering a "plan" to help "rescue" the congregation. I was able to have a brief conversation with them following the service. It became apparent that they did not really have a plan at all. How could they have a plan when they hadn't seen a statement of the monthly expenses or the most recent annual report? It was obvious that they had not done their homework. They had already met with a couple of people from the church who had hopes of somehow reversing the closure decision and bringing renewal to the congregation. They were facing an uphill battle as it was. The ball was rolling toward closure and it would be difficult to stop without causing a lot of damage and hurt.

The decision was made to meet with these folks and to at least let them have their say. At first I thought that it would simply be a courtesy to offer this group a hearing. I soon realized that any effort to listen to this group would be working to undermine the congregation's earlier decision to close. The meeting was scheduled and I asked that a representative from the denomination attend as an observer. After hearing what this group had to say the decision was made to honour the closure process and continue with planning future events. The matter didn't end here, however.

Even though there was some resolution to the immediate closure situation there were a number of things that came out of this effort that were to affect how people subsequently related with each other as we made our way towards the closing service. Seeds had been planted that would eventually complicate an already difficult situation.

A number of years ago I was taking a course on Church transition and was surprised to find that an entire section of this weeklong event was dedicated to conflict. As the situation in my previous congregation developed, and as I thought about the presence of conflict in any changing congregation, this inclusion made a lot of sense. One of my favourite Bible readings is the third chapter of Ecclesiastes and I think that it applies to any discussion on conflict. In this section of Ecclesiastes there is a verse that says, "there is a time for war, and a time for peace."[2]

In many congregations experiencing closure there is often a time for war. There is a time for friction, disagreement and voicing our objections. There is a time for getting angry and rethinking our ideas about people and issues. These are realities that we cannot ignore. We face the challenge of finding some healthy and helpful ways of dealing with those times when people choose war.

Conflict is a word that has assumed a number of negative connotations over the years. We have come to avoid arguments and disagreements because we may feel that we always have to be nice to everyone we encounter in life. When we look more closely, however, we can see that while there are extremes that can cause pain and difficulty, conflict is not always a bad thing. Something healthy and positive can emerge from any open and honest exchange of thoughts, opinions and ideas. Rubbing two sticks together causes enough friction to spark a fire. Fire can destroy. Fire can also bring light and warmth.

Any argument can lead to insights and learnings that help build relationships and help in any decision making process. We have often heard of fistfights in the schoolyard leading to strong friendships. I don't condone violence but we cannot ignore certain realities in human nature. It's as if there is something in our wiring that contributes to disagreement and conflict. There are business leaders who will not make a decision, for example, if their boards are in unanimous agreement on a given issue. Speaking one's mind, within appropriate limits, can help keep the exchange of opinions and ideas flowing. There are many times, however, when conflicts move beyond these limits.

In talking about managing conflict in a congregation, Speed Leas has written, "...if you do it right you can win, stay cool, and collected and amaze your friends and relatives by knowing exactly what to do no matter what happens."[3] Conflict management resources, by their very names, suggest that conflicts can be dealt with to everyone's satisfaction but this isn't necessarily true. Even Jesus tells us there are times in life when we need to "shake the dust from our sandals".[4] As Leas writes, "...to manage means to 'get along', 'make out' or 'muddle through'."[5] Conflicts cannot always be resolved to everyone's satisfaction. Conflicts can be dirty things. When people feel that they are somehow powerless in a conflict situation, they may rely on tactics that are not always healthy in dealing with these disagreements. There may be times when people consider resorting to violence. To continue using the language of Ecclesiastes, there will be a time when people chose war.

One of the main things to beware of when we deal with troubling situations and difficult people is how we respond to them.[6] We will make personal choices between going to war and keeping the peace. Potential arguments and conflicts are all around us. It seems to be a part of life. Church closures provide a tremendous opportunity for people to escalate an already difficult situation. At one extreme, Sam Keen has written about the human need for developing a heroic self-image.[7] There are some who may see a closing congregation as a chance to build this kind of self-image by trying to rescue a congregation in difficulty. These kinds of heroics can complicate the situation in ways that only prolong the pain and difficulty. Anthony Storr discusses the potential for this kind of dynamic when he writes, "The more insecure and helpless a people feel, the more they will look for a savior to rescue them, and a scapegoat to blame for the crisis."[8] Finding a healthy way of responding to these kinds of efforts is important.

We cannot change situations and people. We can only reflect on our own thoughts and behavior. We can only examine our own contributions to a situation. How do we respond, for example, when someone threatens a lawsuit or church discipline? How do we respond when someone calls our competence into question? What do we say? What do we do? Leas writes, "The only person over whom you have any control is yourself, and if you want to deal with the conflict you will have to take the initiative."[9] This is an important point. We are responsible for how we think and feel. We share in the accountability for what happens.

Boers writes, "We often do not know how to be civil and polite and to confront at the same time. By being too nice and passive we allow behavior that would not be tolerated in most other places."[10] Boers goes on to write, "Voluntary organizations sometimes lend themselves to concentrations or abuse of power."[11]

Conflict is something that can have many different levels of intensity. I agree with Kenneth Haugk when he suggests that not everyone in the congregation will be participating in the conflict at the same level of intensity.[12] Some will simply walk away from the entire situation while others will participate fully in the conflict until the bitter end. This was the situation in one congregation in which the closure process displayed many of these levels of intensity. Many of the parishioners wanted to move on and continue their journeys in another congregation. Others combined their efforts in ways that consumed a large amount of time and energy. They filed appeals and detailed complaints against the denomination and staff. Harsh things were said that negatively affected friendships.

Speed Leas names five levels of intensity when it comes to conflicts. There are routine problems that need solving. There are disagreements and contests. There are times when people fight or make a run for it. Finally there are the conflicts labeled "Intractable situations".[13] The challenge in many church closures is that the congregations may experience all five levels of conflict. Level five is the most serious as people carry on as if they were fighting some kind of religious war. They see themselves as fighting for a cause and they may lose sight of the overall situation.

In the summer months of 2003 there were a number of disastrous forest fires in western Canada. One of these fires was threatening the city of Kelowna, British Columbia. Forest fires, earthquakes, and other natural phenomena are ranked using numerical scales. These scales measure the intensity and threat that these situations present. The recent forest fire affecting Kelowna was ranked as a level six. In describing the response to this level six fire Kelowna fire chief Jerry Zimmerman said, "A lot of people don't understand the magnitude a rank 6 fire is: you don't try to put it out. You run from it." There are conflicts that will never be resolved to anyone's satisfaction. There are many conflicts in that the only response is to limit the damage as much as possible and then stand clear as people "duke it out".[14]

If you have ever watched an ice hockey fight you will notice that in most cases the on-ice officials will wait until the players involved fall to the ice exhausted. All too many times people have stepped in while the punches were being thrown and have been injured as a result. There are situations that can only be resolved once the dust settles and people are ready to attempt to sort things out. But not everyone reaches that point at the same time. So much depends on a person's commitment to their particular side of the conflict.

In describing these kinds of dynamics, Jennie Wilting writes that some groups may actually become "attached" to a problem. They get caught up in the situation and can't seem to let go of it.[15] This kind of endless struggle can cause a lot of damage. It can threaten friendships and even end careers. The amount of "collateral damage" can be staggering. It seems all too easy to fall into these levels of conflict but infinitely difficult to find our way out.

Closing a congregation may present a haven for a group of churchgoers Kenneth Haugk has called "antagonists". Haugk writes, "The smaller a congregation is, the more vulnerable it becomes to attack. When dealing with potential antagonists we can follow Jesus' advice and be "as wise as serpents and innocent as doves."[16] There are times when we may think that welcoming and tolerating people who are becoming antagonistic is the "inclusive thing" to do. This kind of thinking is dangerous. Haugk writes, "Letting a small child play with matches or permitting a drunk person to drive a car are most unloving actions. Similarly, allowing antagonists to wreak havoc in the midst, and at the expense of God's people is not loving antagonists or others."[17]

We may not know the amount of damage an individual or group has caused until a conflict has broken out into an open fight. We do not always see the different levels of intensity a conflict can go through before it becomes a serious concern. Borrowing from the work of scholars like Jennie Wilting, I'll briefly outline a few different levels of intensity in this chapter.

The first level of intensity in any conflict is simply solving the problems that happen in life. We can name the difference of opinion over a hymn as an example. This may seem like a trivial situation for us to deal with but small disagreements can often swell into larger and far more destructive ones. It is important to never underestimate the potential for any disagreement to grow and develop.

When it comes to hymn selection we may feel that the first

song on Sunday morning should be new and upbeat. Others may feel that this song should be something more traditional reflecting more of the musical tradition of the faith. These kinds of problems can often be worked out without too much damage. Jennie Wilting writes, "First you need to identify the problem."[18] The respective people can agree that there is a difference of opinion over the kind of music that is needed in opening the Sunday service.

Once you have identified the problem, the second thing to do in this particular example is set a goal. How are we going to deal with a particular problem? A goal will give us something to work toward in coming to an appropriate solution to a problem. When we achieve this goal we will know the problem is close to being solved and that there has been progress. We can know the problem is solved, for example, when a decision has been made about hymn selection and is presented to the person or group leading worship for that particular service.

One simple process by which this problem and goal can be dealt with is for both groups to submit lists of possible hymn selections to a central person for review. The music can be played and people offered a chance to explain their suggestion. This gives people a chance to share their thoughts and opinions. This gives people a chance to listen to each other and also give leaders a sense of the kind of musical tastes currently in the congregation. Once the plan is in place it can be set in motion. The chosen plan may not work so some changes may be needed to improve the process. It is important to measure progress but we cannot expect perfection. Evaluation is important for this reason. Evaluation helps us learn from experience and plan for future possibilities. Regardless of the intensity, evaluation is an important part of dealing with any conflict.

Another thing to remember throughout the effort to solve the problem is the time and energy we have available to carry out these plans and goals.[19] This kind of problem solving can happen within the context of a meeting. It can happen over coffee. It can happen in the minister's office. The main thing is to watch what we say and do. There is also an opportunity to pay careful attention to how we are feeling and what we are thinking. We can track our response as we work at sorting out our disagreement.

This is a simple way of dealing with some of the routine problems experienced within any congregation. It is impossible to expect any group of human beings to plan something without some complications needing to be worked out. This simple process can also be used when dealing with more serious situations. As the intensity of a conflict changes, the amount of time and energy necessary to deal with it will also change. There are times when the clergy and other leaders of a congregation can manage this kind of process. There are times when the situation reaches a level of intensity when even they cannot control what is going on. This is a time when the closure team can be of assistance.

The wider church, through the closure team, may have to step in and share in the work of mediating a conflict within a congregation. The wider church may find itself a part of this conflict and need to turn elsewhere for mediation assistance. One of the things that can help in any kind of conflict of this intensity would be to find out what your respective denomination's conflict resolution process would look like.[20] This will be an important resource for both parishioners and staff. It will also serve as an important resource for the closure team named to work with the congregation.

When entering into mediation it is important to name some ground rules. There has to be a clear exchange of information. This sharing of information can help resolve any confusion or uncertainty because of any rumor that is transmitted along the local grapevine. The groups will also have to identify the importance of confidentiality when preparing for this kind of process. Information may be shared that is potentially harmful to people and their reputation. There may also be information that is simply inaccurate or incorrect and needs to be sorted out. We discuss the importance of the flow of something Boers has called "correct information"[21] in other chapters such as "Planning".

We cannot ignore the potential for conflict in any church closure. I would suggest that the wider church plan for it simply as a precaution. Emotions reach a point where a tremendous amount of heat is generated. Many people tend to act out negatively when they don't have enough power.[22] Sometimes people will have to be told to "get out of the pool" so to speak. This is not some arbitrary use of power and authority by the wider church either. It's a necessary step to prevent the situation from getting worse. The reaction may be potentially explosive. The wider church cannot send one person into this kind of situation alone. Few people have the skill set necessary for this wide-ranging challenge.[23] This is why I recommend the naming of a closure team to assist and share in this kind of work.

Mistakenly sending one person to do the work of a team was something that happened when a particular denomination was assuming the leadership of one congregation's board. There was an assessment made that this particular board was somehow "ineffective". Steps were taken to assign people from outside the congregation to leadership roles. This was interpreted as both a heavy-handed move to take the board's power away and it was also seen as a resource grab. It is difficult for only one person to manage rapidly changing dynamics within a group of people. While one person can possibly manage a leadership role they will certainly need support from teammates and denominational staff. They also need someone watching their back.

In one way the denomination was correct in stepping in to deal with a growing problem. Power had to be taken from a group that had proven they could not manage it. Power had to be re-assigned, or given, to a group who could manage the situation more effectively. Any time this happens it has to be made clear to all why these steps are being taken by the denomination. A rationale has to be offered so that parishioners understand what is happening and the reasons behind these actions. This is another reason why official letters from the denomination to the congregation are so important.

I have mentioned a course in which a section on conflict is a major component. This kind of education is important for any church leader and for the work of the closure team. Courses on conflict management and resolution are available from many sources and any denomination would do well to collect information on these courses for interested people. There may even be paid denominational staff available to offer a course on conflict. Education can help people confront the extremes that conflict may present.

As conflicts reach a point of extreme intensity a lot of emotional energy could be aimed at so called "targets of convenience". People need to focus their energy somewhere and in a constructive manner. We are reluctant to blame ourselves for what has been happening in the congregation so we begin the search for someone else to be a target of our negative energies and blame. These "targets of convenience" may include clergy and other staff. In his book "Church That Works", Gary McIntosh writes, "Critics seek safe targets who will not hurt them in return. Pastors usually do not retaliate."[24] Targets may also include representatives from the wider church or even other parishioners who happen to get caught in the crossfire.[25] Boer has labeled these kinds of situation "fierce landscapes".[26] Leaders have to face tough situations in which they will often find themselves a target. These "fierce landscapes" are places of challenge and difficulty and through which we will have to navigate.

When we experience fierce landscapes there can be the potential for everything from name calling to violence. I have attended meetings in which people were calling one another names like "despicable". This kind of labeling can be dangerous as it affects people in a way that can interfere with their day-to-day lives. Anthony Storr discusses these kinds of dangers when he writes, "...it is when a particular group of human beings is regarded as both dangerous and despicable that we encounter the extremes of human cruelty."[27]

Using labels like "despicable" can lead to more serious behavior later on. Storr goes on to add, "When men (sic) divide the world into good and evil, into sheeps and goats, what happens to the goats is usually horrible."[28] When we use labels we make it all too easy to dismiss the person with whom we are dealing. We may experience the temptation to call someone "crazy", for example, and then simply walk away.[29] This does nothing to clear the air or deal with the problems behind a particular conflict.

We have to watch what we say and do. It is for these reasons that we, as leaders, have to be particularly vigilant of the boundaries we maintain. We have to be careful with the very tone and texture of the way we speak. We have to be careful about the words we choose. The goal is to minimize the ammunition we give people in these kinds of situations. People hold leaders to a high standard and are disappointed when these standards aren't met.

Humans try to build things of lasting value.[30] We cherish the ruins from a variety of ancient cultures. We seem to resist the notion that things come and go. We resist the Hebrew Testament wisdom that there is a certain rhythm that touches our lives. We build something that will one day fall into decay and become a pile of dust. This kind of wisdom can also be applied to the organizations and institutions we create but that eventually fade away. It is difficult to let go when this time approaches, however. It is also difficult to help the people around us accept that it is time to let go. We don't always want to admit that this reality exists. Many of the ancients saw their leaders as being gods of one sort or another. They were crushed when these so-called gods died. We may have inherited some of these same tendencies with the leaders and institutions of our own day. We can see this in how the former Soviets have treated the remains of Lenin.[31] Lenin's remains were preserved and placed behind glass in an ongoing effort to show the value and permanence of his dreams and visions. This reflects the thinking that buildings and people can replace the transcendent in life. This thinking focuses on people and property instead of God.

I think this is one of the reasons why we, as humans, find change so difficult. We have a tendency to resist it. When any organization experiences pain and conflict there is a temptation to make our way back to some sort of "golden age". We want to find our way back to the "good ole days".[32] This is not an option with a church closure. How do we deal with the pain and find a healthy resolution to the situation? We want to contribute to something larger then ourselves. We want to be a part of something that reaches a larger community. Karl Marx expressed this kind of thinking well when he wrote, "I am nothing, and should be everything."[33] We can almost imagine his frustration as we experience these words. Life has limits that we may find difficult to recognize and accept.

So when change does happen we don't always like it and may find we are tempted to work against it. This kind of resistance contributes to the intensity of any conflict. This kind of thinking also keeps us from asking the important questions around God's call for us. We have been challenged in earlier chapters to ask some serious questions about our lives and congregations. These questions help us focus our priorities and commitments in a way that affects our thinking around buildings and people. They help us focus on our need to embrace change as a way of helping us respond to God's call.

We cannot ignore the place of self-image in our response to change and the kinds of conflicts we experience. Jennie Wilting writes, "Another way people create unnecessary problems for themselves is by basing their self worth on the behavior of others."[34] We may experience the temptation to blame a church closure on the quality of clergy leadership that has been offered through the years. The reality is that there may be little or no relationship between the fact that a congregation is closing and the quality of clergy leadership that has been offered. We do not close congregations because clergy did a poor job. Closing the congregation does not mean the lay people did a poor job either. It's all too easy to get defensive when we feel that we are being somehow blamed for what has happened. Some of the things we say and do may contribute to the situation but we cannot blame individual people for causing these kinds of happenings. We can certainly take ownership of what we have done to contribute to a situation but we are not responsible for the things that are beyond our control. We can only be responsible for our own personal thoughts, words, and actions.

One of the realities in any conflict is that we don't always know how people are going to respond to a disagreement. This kind of uncertainty could lead to the increase in the level of fear for many people. As a local closure process drew to a close, people became increasingly anxious about the kinds of behavior they were experiencing at Sunday worship. There were questions being asked about whether or not they would be able to bring their children much longer for fear or exposing them to unacceptable behavior. This fear and uncertainty led to the denomination stepping in and canceling public worship. This is an extreme response but perhaps necessary in some situations. This kind of uncertainty can result in smear campaigns that carry on both within and beyond the congregation. The closure team has to be made aware of these kinds of efforts, as there may be legal and ecclesiastical implications.

Again, if a conflict reaches extreme levels then the wider denomination may need to step in. Decision-making may need to be transferred to the closure team working with the congregation. This may appear to be a little autocratic in some circles but there are times when something drastic needs to be done. Emotions were running so high at my previous congregation that something had to be done or soon people were going to be continually hurt by the words and accusations that were being thrown back and forth. The closure team doesn't have to enjoy this aspect of their work. It's tough, but there are times when this work has to happen.

Another way of looking at church conflict and its effect on congregations is by thinking of the car chases that we see on television. I watch a lot of police shows and there are a usually a number of chases whenever these are aired. The camera puts us in the driver's seat as the squad car takes off after someone trying to make an escape. As the chase develops there are decisions that have to be made quickly. One possibility is to spin the speeding car into the ditch. This kind of maneuver is not the work of an amateur. It doesn't take much to send a speeding car spinning out of control and into the ditch. Sometimes all it takes is a well-placed tap on the fender and the vehicle's speed and momentum will do the rest. A congregation can be proceeding towards closure when something happens that spins everything out of control. When things go off course in this way it becomes almost impossible to return to the original path.

At a recent funeral the eulogist came to the front and announced to the gathered congregation that they would not like what he had to say. He proceeded to identify family issues and offered unwanted advice to individuals named in his eulogy. I quickly realized that something had to be done as people were shouting at him and walking out. I stood up, firmly put my hand on the eulogist's shoulder and told him that these were things that had to be said another time and that he needed to step down. On his way out of the chapel he threw the written eulogy at the family. At this point I realized the service could not be completed as I had planned. Too much had happened to sour the atmosphere. I quickly called for a pause in the service so we could reflect with some quiet music. Things went out of control so quickly that we had to do the best we could to end things whenever we could. This loss of control can happen at any time and in any situation. There are many different ways in which it can happen. Sometimes it's the little things that can do the most damage.

One of these little things can be a simple telephone call or e-mail message. There are a couple of points that I would like to make about these, and other types of communication. My first point is to name the limitations of any e-mail exchange. Electronic mail is a limited medium and it needs to be treated carefully. We can easily over interpret the content of a message. We can find emotions and meaning that may or may not exist. E-mail is a helpful way to communicate routine information and even make plans for lunch. It is not a good way of communicating emotion or capturing the intensity of something we feel a need to say. Use e-mail for routine information sharing only. We can apply this sense of caution to any other media we may access during the closure process.

Another point to keep in mind when dealing with conflict is to state that it is clearly inappropriate to have certain meetings behind closed doors. It is inappropriate, for example, to have board and personnel committee meetings without proper notice or denominational representation. There may be a temptation to gather parishioners with the staff and closure team absent. People may want to discuss issues and clarify potential problems. It is not appropriate to have any committee meetings where people are asked to leave or not invited in the first place. This is especially true when the people being excluded are legally entitled to be present at these meetings. These kinds of meetings happen all too often but we need to remember that any decisions coming out of these meetings are not legal nor are they binding in any way. No one is obligated to meet with any personnel committee if this request came out of an illegal meeting. There are ways of conducting business that follow appropriate channels and we have to honour that.

One of the things that can be remembered in any conflict is the importance of forgiveness. There is an unfortunate old saying that tells us to "forgive and forget". There are dangers in forgetting. If someone harms me in some way I can eventually come to forgive that person. This does not mean that I forget and allow this same harm to happen over and over again. We do others and ourselves no favors by becoming doormats for people to walk upon. Kenneth C. Haugk says this best when he writes, "Be forgiving, but for your congregation's sake, don't be forgetting."[35] There will be a time of forgiveness. There will also be an opportunity to remember so that the amount of pain and conflict in a situation can be reduced.

Remembering the fact that we are all human, as obvious as this may sound, is something that is important for whenever we find ourselves in a situation in which there is conflict.[36] We have to show respect, humanity and compassion when dealing with one another. We all have our hopes and dreams. We all have our commitments and priorities. These important points may go out the window when the situation polarizes and people begin circling the wagons or building camps. By camps I refer to groups of people who share a particular perspective in a given situation. These camps create extreme positions and complicate any kind of healthy response.[37]

We all make decisions in life and congregations are no different. Some of these decisions concern routine matters. Other decisions are far more serious. There is a huge difference, for example, between choosing a staff person and selecting the brand of paper towel to have available in the church kitchen. When decisions are made in the congregation there is a chance that people will take sides on whatever issue is being discussed. Eventually, according to Kenneth Haugk, "...these disagreements can escalate into bitter affairs in which hurt feelings and misunderstandings run rampant. When a conflict requires a decision, some will win and others will lose."[38]

One way to avoid conflict is by following "established policies".[39] Games have rules and manuals exist that can outline these rules so that a game proceeds as smoothly as possible. It's important that we do our homework in becoming familiar with how our respective denomination carries out its business. We have to know the rules. This is called "prevention". It works with forest fires and it can work in congregations. One of the challenges is to identify the limits and norms.

It has been written that, "The conflict free church is a myth and recognizing this can help you adapt to this reality."[40] The main thing is how we work within the disagreements that occur all too frequently in our congregations and in our lives.

Chapter Six Checklist

- Conflict is a reality we all experience in life. This applies to both our individual and congregational lives.
- Not every conflict can be dealt with to everyone's satisfaction.
- When we think that we are in conflict with someone it is helpful to be up front in naming the disagreement.
- Assess the level of conflict and develop a plan to deal with whatever is happening. A plan is helpful for even the smallest disagreements as trust can be built which can come in handy for larger conflicts.
- Consider seeking help from outside sources when confronting extreme conflict.
- Examine the conflict and how you dealt with it. Evaluating your performance is an important way to improve ourselves for the next time we experience conflict.

Endnotes

1. Gary McIntosh "Church That Works" (Grand Rapids, 2004), p. 268
2. Ecclesiastes 3:8
3. Leas, p.12
4. Matthew 10:14
5. Leas, p.12
6. Boers, Arthur P. "Never Call Them Jerks: Healthy Responses to Difficult Behavior" (Bethesda, 1999), p.9
7. Becker, Ernest "The Denial of Death" (New York, 1973), p.xiii
8. Storr, Anthony "Human Destructiveness" (New York, 1991), p.135
9. Leas, p.68
10. Boers, p.19
11. Ibid., p.22
12. Haugk, p.34
13. Boers, p.3
14. "Calgary Herald" September 7th, 2003
15. Wilting, p.12
16. Matthew 10: 16
17. Haugk, p.53
18. Wilting, p.54
19. Ibid., p.55
20. Boers, p.75
21. Ibid., p.86
22, Ibid., p.23
23. Haugk, p.23
24. McIntosh, "Church That Works", p. 269
25. Boers, p.25
26. Ibid., p.7
27. Storr, "Human Destructiveness", p.130
28. Ibid., p.138
29. Boers, p.7

30. Becker, p.5
31. Ibid., p.150
32. Boers, p.110
33. As quoted in Becker, p.265
34. Wilting, p.19
35. Haugk, p.184
36. Ibid., p.36
37. Ibid., p.38
38. Ibid., p.78
39. Ibid., p.94
40. Ibid., p.124

Chapter Seven
Ritual and Liturgy

On August 15th, 2004 an estimated one thousand people gathered for a special mass on the Boston Common. Clergy and lay people from across the Catholic Archdiocese of Boston had assembled to show their strength and solidarity with people affected by the recent closures of roughly seventy area parishes. People came from parishes that were both closing and remaining open. Most of the clergy celebrating the mass were from closing parishes. While some were there to demonstrate against the closures, many others were present to share in the experience of loss and grief.[1]

Closing services, regardless of their style and substance, offer us the opportunity to share our grief and also say "Goodbye". They help us comfort one another. In a recent book, Gene Fowler suggests that bringing comfort in a time of loss and bereavement is one of our priorities.[2] Fowler points to Isaiah 40: 1-11 as an important piece of scripture that helps us understand the place comfort has in our lives. Isaiah writes, "Comfort, comfort my people, says your God." Comforting one another offers the strength and support necessary to help people with the changes happening around them. There are many ways in which we can comfort and support one another. We can help one another in what we say and do. We can help one another in how we plan and carry out the closing service for our congregation.

Closing services that bring comfort and support also help us move on. They can provide a gateway of sorts. Closing services can be compared to funerals. Funerals help us begin the grieving process after a loved one has died. Closing services help us grieve the loss of a congregation. At a recent funeral I was having a conversation with one of the family members of the deceased. At one point of the conversation this family member made the observation, "At least all of that is over with and we can get on with our lives." I wanted to respond to this statement by saying, "Well, yes, sort of, I suppose". This person didn't realize that the actual funeral service was only the beginning of the overall grief process. Our chapter on grief outlined the different aspects of the process. The act of saying "Goodbye" is important. The offering of condolences is an important show of comfort and support for the survivors.

When we think of the times when we have gathered for services such as funerals, we can ask some important questions about the nature of the gatherings themselves. What is ritual? What is a "rite of passage"? It seems that every writer has his or her own definition. For me, perhaps the most effective definition comes from Ronald Grimes in his book entitled "Deeply Into the Bone". Grimes defines rituals, or rites of passage, as "stylized and condensed actions intended to acknowledge or effect a transformation."[3] Carolyn Pogue has written that rituals can be considered "tools for change".[4] Rituals contain words and actions that help us understand what is happening in our lives and the world around us.

Rituals help us experience transition and they also help us stay connected. They help us keep moving through life marking the various stages of our journey. They can provide gateways through which we pass so that we can make our way in the community and in the world. This passage helps us make our way through experiences of loss and grief. Ritual helps us deal with these changing times and how they affect us.

When dealing with the importance of ritual Elaine Ramshaw writes in her book "Ritual and Pastoral Care", "Ritual, in and beyond the church, offers individuals and communities a means to: 1) establish order; 2) make or reaffirm meaning; 3) strengthen the bond of community and 4) address and manage ambivalence."[5] Edgar N. Jackson affirms this need for order when he writes, "The ordered ways of doing things gives us security…. They give meaning and movement to life when those qualities are most needed."[6]

We can see from the above that we address many different needs through ritual.[7] Elaine Ramshaw discusses the connection that can be made between an act of worship and the care we offer people through that act. We may experience the need for forgiveness, for example, and ritual can help us deal with this. If worship doesn't "scratch an itch", so to speak, it is ineffective and empty. It is important, then, that we work to ensure that any ritual is helpful or "healthy".

When considering the importance of healthy ritual Edgar Jackson writes, "A healthy ceremonial is one that provides an appropriate setting in which people can easily express legitimate feelings relating to important events in their lives or in the life of the group."[8] This kind of thinking is consistent with current theory about the importance, and ultimate goals of any ritual that marks a significant loss. Jeanette Auger writes, "There are four functions to most funerals": 1) "They provide a supportive relationship for the bereaved"; 2) "The funeral does the work of reinforcing the reality of death"; 3) "(It's) to make possible the acknowledgement, and open expression of the mourner's feelings of loss and grief and to share these experiences with others"; and 4) "mark the fitting conclusion to the life of one who has died."[9] Auger later adds, "The funeral, then, is a symbolic ritual in every culture that displays change and transformation in human life and death."[10] The two key words to remember are "dignity" and "support". Both are necessary in making ritual effective and meaningful.

It is because of the connection between ritual and pastoral care that Elaine Ramshaw talks about the importance of strong and effective leadership. She writes, "better listeners are potentially better presiders, for they know the needs of their people well."[11] Ramshaw later comments, "The more a minister listens, the more he (sic) will be able to tailor the ritual language to the individual situation."[12] Good liturgy and ritual can begin and nourish important conversations within the community of faith. A person can be reminded of the importance of serving and worshipping God rather than a building, program or staff person.

When we talk about a ritual observing the closure of a congregation it becomes important to use a word like "funeral". As we have previously discussed, we are naming both a loss and the beginning of a grief process. A funeral-type ritual is important for a congregation that is closing. What would this kind of service look like for a closing congregation? What are the hymns and scriptures we would be using? How do we mark the closing of a community of faith that has been important to so many people over the years? How can we possibly do justice to all of the memories and experiences that have been a part of church life in this congregation? These were some of the questions that we confronted as we planned for a closing congregation. Every closing service is going to be unique. There may be an order of service required by the denomination but there will hopefully be opportunity for input by parishioners. People may find certain readings and hymns helpful. The service can be designed to meet the particular needs of a congregation.

One of the first things to keep in mind when planning the closing service is that it cannot be all things to all people. There isn't the time or the energy to meet everyone's needs and expectations. This is a place where compromise becomes important.[13] When we are planning a closing service, we can be aware of the give and take necessary for ensuring that people's needs are respected and that we prioritize what has to happen in order to give people a service that is dignified and effective.

As mentioned earlier we can mark the beginning of the process. We can do our best to get people started on their renewed spiritual journeys. When we close a congregation we are not only saying "Goodbye", we are acknowledging a time of transition in people's lives. Parishioners are moving on to something different and new. They are moving on to new communities of faith where they will relate to people and God in new ways.

Lucy Kolin writes, "In this moment of chaos, and distress, the use of ritual is essential and immediately available to help people of faith make meaning of a reality no one ever planned or imagined for their church."[14] According to Kolin, ritual can also bring the wider church into the picture so that this troubling time can be shared and that the Body of Christ can show its appreciation and thanks for the work and ministry of the closing congregation.

We may not always appreciate or understand the place and value ritual can have in our lives, and in the life of the wider community. When we review the obituaries in the daily newspapers we can see the numerous announcements that include a notation that there will be no funeral service. There may be several reasons why we want to avoid a funeral type service. We may not want to experience the intensity of the emotions, for example, and therefore, will avoid any kind of ritual completely. Funerals are perhaps uncomfortable or depressing for us. We can all too easily forget that we need the opportunity to share a time of loss with others and to share their strength and support. This is a time for community. The absence of a closing service is a lost opportunity to help people begin the work of reflecting on their loss and to move on.

It is important to remember in this kind of closing ritual that God will not abandon us. The United Church of Canada Creed states, "God is with us, we are not alone." These are important words to carry with us as we go through the closing process. Knowing that God is with us can be a sense of divine companionship that gives us strength as we face what lies ahead. We can also stress God's strength and permanence in a closing service. We have previously experienced the words of Isaiah 40: 1-11 in another context. We can also consider the prophet's words in this part of our discussion. Isaiah talks about the brief and uncertain life span we have as human beings. We are compared to grass that grows and withers within a season. Isaiah writes in verse eight, "The grass withers, the flower fades; but the word of the Lord will stand forever." People come and go but God is that one presence remaining through all time. We can also apply this thinking to the organizations and institutions we create as individuals and communities.

Ritual can happen in times of worship. This ritual can include hymn sings and celebrations of Holy Communion. We can pour water from the baptismal font or simply break something.[15] The act of sharing a meal can also be a ritual act. This is an important part of planning any closing service. There are a number of possibilities to consider when looking ahead. In the early stages of the planning process we can include efforts to plan a feast of some sort. Members of the congregation can plan to hire caterers to prepare and serve the meal. This would free up the people who would normally be doing the work of putting on the supper. Everyone can then have a chance to share in the final goodbyes and thanksgivings. Another possibility is that people from other congregations could organize and serve a closing supper for a congregation that they have been working with over the years. This would be a tangible show of support and care for the people of a closing congregation.

When planning a closing worship it may be a good idea to

plan an entire weekend of events so that there are a number of opportunities for people to remember and offer thanks. There would be a number of opportunities to look ahead to what the future will bring. If a large number of people are transferring to one or two congregations then the clergy and lay people from these neighboring congregations can participate in some meaningful way as well. There can be a time of welcome and invitation. There can be a time when these new faces can simply be a helpful presence through the weekend activities. It may be a meaningful touch to include hymns and readings that were offered when the closing church was originally opened and dedicated. This historical kind of documentation is not always available but when it is, there can be a real strength to including the relevant hymns and readings.

This notion of scheduling the closing rituals of a congregation over a weekend is consistent with the practice of the Russian Orthodox Church. Ramshaw writes, "We can learn a lesson from the Russian Orthodox, who have a two-part ritual for the dead: an evening service for mourning and eulogy, followed by a vigil, and a morning mass of the resurrection."[16] This may be a helpful order when planning the closing service for a congregation. There can be a meal on the Saturday evening, for example, followed by a Sunday service. It may be helpful to schedule the service for an afternoon time as lay people and clergy from within the denomination may find a morning service difficult to attend. This can allow the congregation to gather that Sunday morning for a personal service that can include meaningful hymns and prayers.

Former clergy can be invited to closing services as well. They can offer some valuable stories, memories and insights into the gifts that the people and congregation have shared with a denomination and community. At one closing service I attended some of the former clergy had a chance to share some of their stories and memories. One of the former ministers even wrote a hymn to mark the occasion. This was a special offering that gave the occasion an added significance.

Denominational officials may be important participants in any closing service. In some denominations it may be a requirement. If a denomination is built around an hierarchy including bishops, for example, then these Bishops may be required to lead the closing service. Lay and clergy leaders from a denomination can share in the service leadership as a way of showing the connection between the closing congregation and the wider church. They can also show the care and concern the wider church has for the people of the closing congregation. These officials can lead the service or they can participate in any of the different elements contained within the service. Community leaders can also be invited to attend the closing service.

One of the elements that could be included in any closing service is something called the "Communion of Fire". My first experience with this ritual was at a local Unitarian church. It was the service before New Year's Eve and people were being offered the opportunity to examine the year that was coming to a close. They were invited to think about the good times and the challenges. People were then given the opportunity to write their cares and concerns on a piece of paper. They were also asked to add their regrets and reflections if they would find that helpful. When these notes had been written the people came forward and lit their slips of paper from the Christ candle. With these pieces of paper ablaze they placed them in a large metal bowl. Burning the paper symbolized letting go of the past and seeing the need for moving into the future without the baggage of the past.

The same type of ritual can be planned for a closing service. This can be an important moment when we name the thoughts and feelings that have accompanied us on our congregation's journey to closure. It is also a moment when we can let go of these thoughts and feelings so that we can move into the future without the spiritual baggage that can only weigh us down. This can be an important way of symbolically bringing closure to any kind of conflict that had been developing through the closure process.

One of the things that make rituals such as the Communion of Fire so important is that they touch us in ways that meals and meetings cannot. Abraham Heschel has written, "Spiritual problems cannot be solved by administrative techniques."[17] Sometimes all it takes to communicate something is a simple gesture or piece of music. The simple act of burning something we have written on a piece of paper can mean a lot when it comes time to say "Goodbye". Sometimes a pattern on a banner can express people's thoughts and emotions. These kinds of intangibles are not age specific either.

As we talk about the importance of ritual and worship we cannot forget the place of young people in any congregation. Planning efforts can include their contributions as well. They may be asking questions that can be addressed by the planning team and worship leaders. People of all ages will be experiencing this loss in one way or another so it is important to include them whenever possible. Their ways of grieving may differ but that does not mean they can be excluded or ignored. One way in which we can share in the closing ceremonies is by helping create a banner that can be hung in one of the congregations people will be moving to. The young people could also be given the opportunity to create personal banners they can take with them to their new congregations. This is important in areas where people may not be moving to the same congregation.

The closure team can assist people planning a closing service. Their participation can be as active or limited as the congregation would like. They could represent the denomination in any effort to decommission property that may have been used by the congregation. They can participate as guest speakers or preachers. They may have access to music and material that the planning team does not. It is important that the closure team be included in any planning effort, if only for people and resources they can access. They may also have experience and insights that can help the worship leaders reach out and touch those attending the closing service.

Whatever we say and do in the time leading up to the closing service we have to address the thoughts and feelings of the gathered people. We need to address their innermost searching in this time of loss and grief. As a congregation makes its way through the closing process there is no time or need for "Bring a Friend" Sundays. There is no real need to introduce new hymns or hymn books unless there is a direct application to the closing process. Introducing a hymn like "In the Bulb There is a Flower" can be helpful and meaningful. Introducing music simply because it is trendy is not really helpful, nor is it relevant. There will be a time to learn new music when people choose their new faith communities. The main goal of this kind of service, as Edgar N. Jackson writes, is to help a person "carry their burdens with courage".[18]

In carrying our "burdens with courage", an important goal to keep in mind for any closing service is the expression of the faith that has nourished the congregation throughout its history.[19] This belief has nourished and sustained a given community of faith. This faith can be shared through bible readings and prayers. This faith can be reflected in the hymns selected and the themes chosen to run through the service. There can be a time when people can offer their memories of when the collective faith of a congregation has helped touch the community around the church. At one closing service a former minister talked about the kinds of community organizations that shared the church facilities with the congregation. He talked about the outreach programs that were developed. He talked about the people whose lives were improved and about the meals and the networking. These are all important things to remember and offer in the closing service.

An interesting possibility for this kind of sharing is in the testimony that community people can offer. These people can share something of how the congregation reached out and helped others. One congregation set up a storefront operation helping people develop job skills to help them build better lives. Another congregation set up literacy classes for young people having trouble learning to read. We don't always know the kind of effect we have on others until they take the time to tell us. It's important to hear these things when we confront the closing of our congregation. It's important to know that our efforts have made a difference in the lives of individuals and the wider community.

One of the helpful ways in which we can experience the ministry a congregation has provided is by creating a kind of collage or "photo-quilt". David Kuhl writes, "Our families are like a quilt. Each of us sees and experiences something unique to which we are. Whenever a child is born, it's a different family. The dynamics have changed immediately."[20] Just as people have made quilts out of different shapes and colours, congregations can reflect this same kind of variety as well. Photo-quilts can be displayed so that people can share in the memories. They can see the faces and activities contributing to the life of the congregation. They can relive the experiences and encounters giving the congregation such an important place in their lives. Building this kind of display could be an important activity leading up to the closing weekend.

As we have been discussing, the closing of a church can be observed in a final act of worship in which we remember and offer thanks for the life of the congregation. The time leading up to the final service can be another way of observing the closure. As the closing process works its way towards the final service, preparations can include looking ahead to what happens in weekly worship. As people prepare for the congregation's closure, prayers and devotions can help point to some of the themes and content that will be within the final service itself. Worship leaders can build on scripture readings included in their respective denomination's lectionary. Leaders can also add whatever readings they feel would be important for parishioners to experience. There can also be devotionals before meetings that name things like loss and grief and how this will affect the congregation. These are also times in which information can be shared and questions asked. One church board took time during the announcements in Sunday worship when they offered updates to the gathered people. This kind of effort is consistent with our earlier discussion of the importance of sharing clear and accurate information.

In saying this, there can be an opportunity to schedule several hymn sings so that people can share in singing the hymns that have been a meaningful part of life and worship throughout the congregation's history. There can be a plan to sing a selected number of pieces and there can also be an opportunity for people to request their favourites. In a congregation that I previously served there were opportunities at the beginning of worship to sing some selections requested by the congregation. This was an opportunity for people to request their old favourites that were not sung often since we were trying to introduce newer types of music. People came away from those services assured that their favourites were not being forgotten.

Music is an important way for people to tap into their grief so this kind of hymn selection and singing is critical. If the music people are still on board then their input is important. They know what people in the congregation have come to find meaningful and helpful through the years. Even if there is a change in music leadership an effort can still be made to meet the varied musical needs of parishioners. This is an important way of reaching out and caring for a group of grieving people.

Perhaps the key word to keep in mind is "remember". As we move into the future we can carry the memory of the closing congregation in our hearts and minds. As we plan the closing service we can consider including this one important word whenever we can. We can offer prayers, read scriptures and sing hymns. We can also remember. When the local Roman Catholic bishop participated in a closing mass, one of the things he did was to stress the importance of remembering. He would make his way around the sanctuary and stop at various places. When he paused at these places he would remind worshippers to "remember the past". When he stopped at the baptismal font, for example, he would urge the gathered people to remember all of the times this important sacrament was celebrated and the people who were touched by this opportunity.[21] Inviting people to remember offers an important opportunity to continue the process of reflecting on, and articulating the place of the congregation in their lives. Inviting people to remember is an important way of listening to and caring for them.

As we try and care for the congregation facing closure we can consider the possibility of holding healing services and conversations as people make their way through this process. I have mentioned this before and it might be helpful to repeat it here. There may be a need for spontaneous sharing and prayer. People can share their thoughts, stories, and feelings. We had some of these services at one of my previous congregations and we invited the pastoral care worker from our denomination. She had become acquainted with some of the parishioners and wanted to share these healing times with them.

In the time leading up to the church closure there will be worship opportunities that cannot be missed. Kolin writes, "for every worship service that precedes the final service, the preacher needs to preach in a way that encourages honesty, repentance, mutual consolation, and faith in God's provenance and Easter."[22] In other words, given the fragile state of the congregation, we need to deal with certain issues if we are to minister to the people in the pews. We can anticipate these needs and issues when we do our long range planning. We may need to deal with the surprises that continue emerging as we make our way to the closing service.

When dealing with any surprises that confront us we cannot allow the situation to become any more stressful for parishioners than it already is. There is an important line in the doctor's Hippocratic oath that we can apply in this situation and that is the one calling on a physician to "do no harm". However, when harm does come to a congregation then we have to deal with it. Whether that means intervention from the wider church or something that the minister needs to do, there is something that needs to happen. This kind of intervention may happen during the planning effort for the closing service. A rapidly changing situation may affect what is said and done. It may also affect the timing of the services and activities people can share. In this case, the closure team should be ready to take over at any time. The closure team will have an important trouble-shooting role in these situations. The closure team and parishioners would then have to do their best to plan the service, or services, in a way that is consistent with as many of the congregational members wishes as possible.

There is an old phrase that says we should "never speak ill of the dead". This thinking can affect how we mark the end of a congregation. We may face the temptation to sanctify it and make it out to be something that it has never been. We can celebrate the positive and good things. We may face the temptation to stop there and ignore the negative. We have to be realistic. How do we include both the positive and negative in our rituals and liturgies? The key is to be honest and work hard at concentration on what people need to experience as they make their way into a new and hopeful future.

Chapter Seven Checklist

- Who will organize and lead the final worship service? Will representatives from the denomination be invited to participate in the planning process?
- Who will participate in this closing service? Who will preach? Who will lead the music?
- Will previous clergy leaders and staff people be invited to attend and participate in this closing service?
- What, if any, roles will the denomination play in the closing service? Will there be any involvement in planning the closing service? Will there be any leadership from denominational officials in this closing service?
- Are there any prescribed rituals or requirements for the closing service? Does the denomination have an order of service, for example, that is required for any closure service? Is there something we have to do or say?
- Will there be a reception following the closing service? Who will organize and assist in preparing this reception?

Endnotes

1. "Boston Catholics Gather for Mass in Response to Parish Closures", Catholic News Service, I-observe website
2. Fowler, Gene "Caring Through the Funeral" (St. Louis, 2004), p. 148 ff
3. Grimes, Ronald L. "Deeply Into the Bone" (Berkley, 2000), p. 6
4. Pogue, p.19
5. Quoted in "Ending With Hope", p. 135
6. Jackson, "For the Living", p.93)
7. Ramshaw, p.16
8. Jackson, "For the Living", p.38)
9. Auger, p.154

10. Ibid., p.154
11. Ramshaw, p.18
12. Ibid., p.56
13. Grimes, p.240
14. "Ending With Hope", p. 135
15. Grimes, p.220
16. Ramshaw, p.35
17. Heschel, p.103
18. Jackson, "Understanding Grief", p.221
19. Ibid., p.221
20. Kuhl, p.85
21. "Western Catholic Reporter" July 16th, 2001. This part of the liturgy seems to be based largely on resources prepared by the Archdiocese of Chicago. Some of these materials can be found in the February / March 1996 issue of Liturgy 90 circulated by the Archdiocese of Chicago's Liturgy Training Publications.
22. "Ending With Hope", p.142

Conclusion
Hopes and New Beginnings

An ancient Gaelic proverb says, "An end will come to the world, but music and love will endure."[1] The closing service is the end of our work. Or is it? In his poem, "Little Giddings" T.S. Elliot has written, "The ending is where we start from". Abraham Heschel offers a similar insight when he writes, "Death, then, is not simply man's coming to an end. It is also entering a beginning."[2] When the early Scottish settlers came to North America they grieved the land they had left behind. They missed the people and the mountains. They had no idea what was going to happen in their new surroundings. As they moved through their early experiences in their new home an interesting thing happened. Their grief gave way to hope.[3] These thoughts around endings; new beginnings and eternity are echoed in many different religious traditions. The Buddha once said, "Decay (change) is inherent in all component things but the truth will remain forever!"[4]

Death can be seen as a doorway or gateway in which we are moving from one reality to another. Death is a reality we cannot ignore. This is true of congregations as well as individual human beings. A colleague once wrote, "If God leads us to build church buildings, God can lead us to close them. Both can be faithful and both can be life giving."[5] When the decisions are made and the closure process unfolds an important journey has begun.

This journey through life and rebirth is consistent with the timeless story we share as a church. The Christian story reaches a place where it experiences the realities and opportunities of Good Friday and Easter Morning. Good Friday is that time when we remember the death of Jesus Christ. We make our way through the execution and burial. We emerge on Easter morning with the resurrection.

The key to this entire movement is the combination of Good Friday and Easter morning. We can't have one without the other. It would be all too easy to avoid Good Friday and wait for Easter morning. All too many of us face this temptation. We cannot yield to this temptation, however. New life and resurrection cannot happen without the experience of death. In Matthew's Gospel Jesus says, "For those who want to save their life will lose it, and those who lose their life for my sake will find it."[6] This saying can apply to individuals and it can also apply to congregations.

A number of years ago I was serving a congregation in northern Alberta. The aging hospital building in our community was being replaced by a new structure and was to be torn down. As the building was being torn down some of the bricks and other building materials were being set aside. These materials would eventually find their way into the construction of a new church building in our community. For many of us this simple act of renewal stood as a symbol of how the realities of death and resurrection can come together in some meaningful way.

Throughout this book one of the themes that we have been dealing with has been this reality of death and resurrection. In any church closure we may reach a point where we face the closure of a congregation and also work at finding a way to move on. Ernest Becker has written, "If there is tragic limitation in life there is also possibility. What we call maturity is the ability to see the two in some kind of balance into which we can fit creativity."[7] All too often we focus so much energy on the closure, itself, that we cannot see what lies ahead. We cannot see the new relationships and possibilities. We cannot see the new connections and opportunities for serving one another. We focus so much of our energy on Good Friday we fail to see the Easter moment ahead.

One searching question that is asked at a time of loss and grief is "What sort of good can come from the death of those we love?"[8] We can ask the same question when a congregation closes. How can we bring new life out of this kind of loss? In considering these kinds of questions Neimeyer and Anderson offer three possibilities. The first is that family and friends can take advantage of the opportunity to renew the bonds that hold them together. We can find new ways of relating and building the connections we have. This can happen in a new congregation. We can also find common interests granting us new social possibilities. One family, for example, has made an annual tradition of a fall turkey supper held by their church. One way of maintaining this "tradition" can be the search for another supper in which they can attend each year. They can also create a time of their own when people can gather and share a meal together.

The second possibility that Neimeyer and Anderson offer is that we can "develop a greater compassion for others". We can seek out new ways of investing our energies. We can find new commitments that help match our gifts and skills with needs in the community. This would ideally happen within the context of a congregation. This could also happen, however, in a social organization as well. The main thing is that we find a way of connecting with the community around us. These new connections will help us deal with the grief that can happen when our congregation closes. This will help us meet new people and replace the relationships that may have been lost with the congregation's closure.

Finally, the third possibility that we can consider is to develop an even stronger spirituality. A declining congregation can only offer a limited range of possibilities for worship and building our relationship with God. When we begin the search for a new congregation we can find out what is available for worship. We can consider our likes and dislikes when it comes to music and worship style. We can seek out new ways of listening for, and responding to God's voice in our lives. This can be an interesting and potentially exciting opportunity. It's an opportunity that can lead to a renewed faith and a growing relationship with the wider body of Christ.

In building hope in a new beginning we can look forward to seeing what is around the corner. We can experience optimism in knowing that these new opportunities can help us build our relationship with God and God's wider church. It's a frustrating reality of being human that we do not know what lies ahead but this could be a good thing. Will we find friendship and community in our new congregations? Will we find new life? We have to move forward and make new discoveries for ourselves.

Bridges writes in his book on transitions, "First there is an ending, then a beginning, with an important empty and fallow time in between".[9] What will this empty and fallow time look like for the people and leaders of a closing congregation? We may be referring to the search that begins when the doors close. We may be referring to the time when we seek out a new congregation. We may be talking about that time when we reconsider our social and ministry needs. Perhaps we can word this question another way by quoting the Psalmist when they write, "How can we sing the Lord's song in a strange land?"[10]

As people move through the "strange land" referred to by the Psalmist, follow up will be important. We can check in and find out where people have gone. We can ask how they are doing. We can make contact with clergy in these congregations to see how the new relationship is developing. People who seem to be adrift may need some pastoral contact. This is where the work of pastoral care givers can be complicated. Not everyone will want this kind of attention as they may want to simply fade into the background. Many will simply want to be left alone.

Pastoral contact and follow-up can be one of the closure team's continuing tasks once the closure has been completed. They can do this on behalf of the wider church and it may be a helpful way of demonstrating ongoing care and concern. There can be people so disgusted with a closure that they want nothing to do with a denomination ever again, and of course, they are free to make this choice. We may not agree with these kinds of decisions but we still have to honour them.

This pastoral contact may be limited to finding out how people are doing in their new congregations. People may need the assurance that it is understandable if they do not feel an immediate need to participate in the life and the leadership of these new congregations. There may be a period of time when they need to grieve and develop some level of comfort with their new surroundings. Some may want to jump in with both feet. Have they made new friends? Have they met the parishioners of these new congregations? The clergy from the closing congregations may need to make contact with colleagues in order to facilitate contact with people in these new, and potentially unfamiliar congregations. One helpful piece of advice is that people not do anything in their new congregations for at least a year. This will allow them to build a sense of belonging. This will allow their roots to take hold and begin a new time of growth and development.

We can also be aware that groups from the closed church will continue to meet. This is something that will happen whether we want it to or not. People will meet for a variety of reasons. They will meet for worship and Bible Study. They may try to maintain that sense of community that had been established within the congregation. These groups will be creative in their search for space in which they can arrange their meetings. There is a church building that was sold and converted into an inner city library.[11] It may be helpful to suggest places where groups could go for their social meetings, Bible studies, etc.

The priority in all of these pastoral needs is that we find and build community. We need to find a place where we can develop a sense of belonging. This sense of belonging is what helps maintain our bonds with the wider body of Christ. Heschel has written of the Jewish people, "Judaism exists only in community. The primary concern of the Jew is ... that he assure the continued existence of the people of Israel."[12] As Christians, we can consider the same calling. We are called to build community, both as local congregations and as the wider Body of Christ. When the congregation closes we can continue a response to the higher call. We can experience a call to a new community where we can build a new life and a new hope. We can maintain relationships from our previous congregation and we can build on contacts with a new spiritual community.

One of the important realities that we can keep in mind throughout this entire closing process is that we do not experience this alone. We can be reminded that, as the creed of the United Church of Canada states, "God is with us" and "we are not alone". God is with us when the decisions are made around whether or not a congregation closes. God is with us through the difficult work of closing these congregations. God is with us when we grieve the loss of a congregation. God is also with us as we move on to new communities and new opportunities. As a Scottish bard once wrote after arriving in North America, "Since every pursuit that once I turned my enthusiasm so keenly to has now been left behind me, it's time for me to pray more often and stand close to God."[13]

Endnotes

1. Dunn, Charles W. "Highland Settler: A Portrait of the Scottish Gael in Nova Scotia" (Toronto, 1953, 1980), p.37
2. Heschel, p.367
3. Dunn, p. 24
4. Kramer, p. 200
5. Holmes, Karen "Closing Churches: The Bawlf-Daysland Experience" in "Exchange" Winter 1993, p.13
6. Matthew 16: 25
7. Becker, p.266
8. Thompson, P.49
9. Bridges, p.18
10. Psalm 137
11. Desantis, Solange "Whither the Downtown Montreal Churches" in the 'Anglican Journal' May 2003
12. Heschel, p.65
13. Dunn, p.91

Bibliography

—"The Essential Jung: Selected Writings" Ed. Anthony Storr. Princeton University Press (Princeton, New Jersey), 1983.

—"The Letters of the Younger Pliny" Betty Radice, Transl. Penguin (London, England), 1969 Ed.

-Anderson, Terence R. "End of Life Decisions" in Touchstone. January 2003.

-Arn, Win "Pastor's Manual for Effective Ministry" Church Growth (Monrovia, California), 1988

-Auger, Jeanette A. "Social Perspectives On Death and Dying" Fernwood (Halifax, N.S.), 2000

-Bannister, Jerry "Whigs and Nationalists: The Legacy of Judge Prowse's 'History of Newfoundland'" Acadiensis (Autumn, 2002), p.84-109

-Barker, Ralph. "The Royal Flying Corps in World War One", Constable and Robinson (London, England), 2002 Ed.

-Becker, Ernest. "The Denial of Death", Simon and Schuster (New York, N.Y.), 1973.

-Bennis, Warren and Nanus, Bert. "Leadership" Harper Collins (New York, N.Y.), 1985, 1997

-Berger, Peter "Invitation to Sociology: A Humanistic Perspective". Anchor Books (Garden City, N.Y.), 1963

-Berger, Peter "The Noise of Solemn Assemblies" Doubleday and Company, Inc (Garden City, N.Y.), 1961

-Boers, Arthur P. "Never Call Them Jerks: Healthy Responses To Difficult Behavior". The Alban Institute (Bethesda, Maryland), 1999.

-Bridges, William. "Transitions". Addison Wesley (Reading, Massachusetts), 1980

-Copp, Terry and Bill McAndrew. "Battle Exhaustion: Soldiers and Psychiatrists in the Canadian Army, 1939-1945". McGill—Queen's University Press (Kingston, Ontario), 1990.

-Derrida, Jacques. "The Work of Mourning" Ed. And Translated by Pascale-Anne Brault and Michael Naas. Chicago and London: University of Chicago Press, 2001

-Desantis, Solange "Whither the Downtown Montreal Churches" in the Anglican Journal, May, 2003

-Drucker, Peter "Innovation and Entrepreneurship" Harper and Row (New York, N.Y.), 1985

-Dudley, Carl. "Where Have All The People Gone?" Pilgrim Press (New York, N.Y.), 1979.

-Dunn, Charles W. "Highland Settler: A Portrait of the Scottish Gael In Nova Scotia". University of Toronto Press (Toronto, Ontario), 1953, 1980 Edition.

-"Ending With Hope". Ed. By Beth Anne Gaede. The Alban Institute (Bethesda, Maryland), 2002

-Flood, Gavin. "An Introduction to Hinduism". Cambridge University Press (Cambridge, England), 1999 (Ed.)

-Fowler, Gene "Caring Through the Funeral" Chalice Press (St. Louis Missouri), 2004

-Friedrich, R.E. and Oswald, R.M. "Discerning Your Congregation's Future" The Alban Institute (Bethesda, Maryland), 1996

-Frye, Northrop. "The Educated Imagination" Indiana University Press (Bloomington, Illinois), 1964

-Goleman, Daniel et al. "Primal Leadership: Realizing the Power or Emotional Intelligence". Harvard Business School Press (Boston, Massachusetts), 2002

-Graham, John "Outdoor Leadership: Technique, Common Sense and Self-Confidence" Mountaineers (Seattle, Washington), 1997

-Grant, John Webster "George Pidgeon: A Biography" The Ryerson Press (Toronto, Ontario), 1962

-Grimes, Ronald L. "Deeply Into the Bone: Re-inventing Rites of Passage" University of California Press (Berkley, California), 2000

-Harland, Gordon. "Engaging the Issues Before Us With Confidence and Hope" in Touchstone. January 2003

-Haugk, Kenneth C. "Antagonists In the Church". Augsburg Publishing House (Minneapolis, Minnesota), 1988

-Hemmingway, Ernest. "The Old Man and the Sea". Scribner Classic (New York, N.Y.), 1986 Edition.

-Heschel, Abraham. "Moral Grandeur and Spiritual Audacity", Ed. Susan Heschel. Noonday Press (New York, N.Y.), 1996.

-Holmes, Karen "Closing Churches: The Bawlf-Daysland Experience" in Exchange, Winter 1993, p.10-13

-Ironside, Virginia "You'll Get Over It" Penguin (London, England), 1997

-Jackson, Edgar N. "Understanding Grief" Abingdon Press (Nashville, Tennessee) 1957

-Jackson, Edgar N. "For The Living" Channel Press (Des Moines, Iowa), 1963

-Jones, Ezra Earl. "Strategies for New Churches" Harper and Row (New York, N.Y.), 1976

-Kramer, Kenneth "The Sacred Art of Dying: How World Religions Understand Death" Paulist Press (Mahwah, New Jersey), 1988

-Kristeva, Julia "Black Sun: Depression and Melancholia". Columbia University Press (New York, N.Y.), 1987, 1989 Edition.

-Kuhl, David. "What Dying People Want" Doubleday Canada (Toronto, Ontario), 2002

-Kuhn, Thomas. "The Structure of Scientific Revolutions" University of Chicago Press (Chicago, Illinois), 1962, 1970.

-Leas, Speed B. "Leadership and Conflict". Abingdon (Nashville, Tennessee), 1982

-Lencioni, Patrick. "The Five Temptations of a C.E.O." Jossey-Bass (New York, N.Y.), 1998

-Malphurs, Aubrey "Planting Growing Churches for the Twenty-First Century" (2nd Ed.) Baker Books (Grand Rapids, Michigan), 1998

-Marty, Martin Ed. "Death and Birth of the Parish" Concordia Publishing House (St. Louis, Missouri), 1964

-May, Rollo. "Power and Innocence: A Search for the Sources of Violence" Norton (New York, N.Y.), 1972

-McIntosh, Gary L. "Biblical Church Growth" Baker Books (Grand Rapids, Michigan), 2003

————, "Church That Works" Baker Books (Grand Rapids, Michigan), 2004

-Merkin, Daphne "Dreaming Of Hitler: Passions and Provocations" Harcourt Brace and Company (New York, N.Y.), 1997

-Murray-Parkes, Colin "Bereavement: Studies of Grief In Adult Life". Penguin (London, England), 1998

-Pogue, Carolyn "Language of the Heart: Rituals, Stories, and Information". Northstone Publishing (Kelowna, B.C.), 1998

-Ramshaw, Elaine. "Ritual and Pastoral Care". Fortress Press (Philadelphia, Pennsylvania), 1987

-Riegel, Christian. "Writing Grief: Margaret Laurence and the Work of Mourning". University of Manitoba Press (Winnipeg, Manitoba), 2003.

-Robertson, Heather "Meeting Death: In Hospital, Hospice and At Home" McClelland and Stewart (Toronto, Ontario), 2000

-Sacks, Oliver "The Man Who Mistook His Wife for a Hat: And Other Clinical Tales" Harper Perennial (New York, N.Y.), 1970, 1990 Edition.

-Sandys, Celia and Littman, Jonathan "We Shall Not Fail: The Inspiring Leadership of Winston Churchill" Portfolio (New York, N.Y.), 2003

-Schaller, Lyle "Tattered Trust: Is There Hope For Your Denomination?" Abingdon Press (Nashville, Tennessee), 1996

-Storr, Anthony. "Human Destructiveness" Ballantine Books (New York, N.Y.), 1991

-Swanson, Eric "Good To Great Congregations" in Leadership, Spring 2003

-Tolstoy, Leo. "Resurrection". Oxford University Press (New York, N.Y.), 1999 Ed.

-"Loss and Grief: A Guide for Human Services Practitioners"
Ed. By Neil Thompson. Palgrave Press (New York, N.Y.),
2002

-Whalley, Lawrence. "The Aging Brain" Columbia University
Press (New York, N.Y.), 2001.

-Wilting, Jennie "Nurse, Colleagues and Patients: Achieving
Congenial Interpersonal Relationships" University of Alberta
Press (Edmonton, Alberta), 1990